Iron Eyes

RORY BLACK

A Black Horse Western

ROBERT HALE · LONDON

ISBN 0 7090 6480 2

Robert Hale Limited
Clerkenwell House
Clerkenwell Green
London EC1R 0HT

ALS ? MI¢

Photoset in North Wales by
Derek Doyle & Associates, Mold, Flintshire.
Printed and bound in Great Britain by
WBC Book Manufacturers Limited, Bridgend

dedicated to
Laura and Jack

ONE

The Red Dog Saloon had seen its fair share of trouble and bloodshed over the years, but nothing like this. This had been a blood-bath, resulting in total destruction.

The crimson blood was still streaming down the expensively papered walls as the choking gunsmoke began to clear. Death lay all around this place. Screams from the saloon's dancing girls echoed off the wooden walls as the gaunt, tall man slowly moved across the body-littered floor.

He held tightly on to his still-smoking Navy Colts as he moved forward amid the carnage. His worn boots stuck to the fresh red liquid as he headed for the swing doors.

The man had a haunting face that hid beneath long, limp, black hair. He wore a battered, weather-proof coat favoured by long riders and road agents which almost reached his spurs. With each stride the sound of bullets clinking together in his deep pockets filled the room.

7

This was no normal man. This was an evil spirit who had yet to die and seek refuge in Hell. Stepping over bodies, he studied the scene with an almost disconcerting lack of interest. This was a man who wore no gunbelt like average folks did. His broad pants belt doubled for holsters.

Pushing his way through the swing doors of the Red Dog, the tall man stuffed both his pistols into his belt and stopped to watch the crowd that was rushing toward him. The sight of this stranger stopped every single man, woman and child in their tracks.

Even the town sheriff, clutching his trusty Winchester, found himself staggering to a complete halt by the very sight of the man on the boardwalk.

It was dusk and getting darker with every heartbeat as the tall, evil-looking creature pushed a long, thin cigar between his dry, cracked lips. As he struck the match down along the wooden upright and cupped the flame around the tip of his smoke, the true extent of this stranger's features became apparent to all the watching townspeople.

This was a cold face. An evil face. The face of a man who survived on rotgut whiskey rather than solid food.

He had cold eyes of a colour that resembled hammered gun metal in their deadness. The eyes were how everyone knew who it was.

This was the legendary bounty hunter known simply as 'Iron Eyes'.

They all watched as the thin leg forced his boot into his stirrup, and he eased himself off the boardwalk into his waiting saddle. Blowing the thick ash from his cigar, he turned the dark grey horse toward the crowd of people and rode slowly at them. As if instructed by a silent voice, they all parted and allowed him clear passage out of their town.

The sheriff stared helplessly up at the lifeless face that returned his glare.

The cold, deep-set pupils burned into the lawman.

As Iron Eyes spurred his mount, the long black hair beat up and down upon his collar.

It was like the flapping of a bat's wings.

TWO

Leaving the bodies back in the Red Dog posed no problems for the rider as he headed deeper and deeper into the dark prairie. Why he killed so many innocent people was a question he failed to ask himself.

Someone had made a mistake and he had been taught a lesson. As often happens in small towns, the victim had a friend who also had to be shot.

Iron Eyes had been drawn on and responded with his usual deadly accuracy. When he had finished killing the fools he had only one bullet left in his Navy Colts.

The reason why he was in Arizona was simply business. He had plucked a wanted poster off a wall outside a sheriff's office back in Dodge, and wanted the twenty thousand dollars for bringing in a certain Dan Hardy. Dead or alive suited Iron Eyes just fine.

In fact, it was the real reason he had set out

10

upon this long trek that had lasted over two months. He could almost smell the money and the blood as he rode.

Iron Eyes used every drop of the full moon to aid his ride through the cold night as he headed toward the next town on the stage route.

Rio Drago was where Iron Eyes hoped his quest would end. He knew that soon he would be running out of places to go. The tall, arid mountains seemed almost blue as he rode through the silent valley.

Faster and faster he forced his horse to race. He did not like this part of the world and would not risk camping out unless he could not avoid it.

This was the land of the whip scorpion and diamond-back rattlers. Iron Eyes spurred his horse on. He would not stop until he had reached the distant township of Rio Drago. There he would rest and wait for his prey.

As the sun rose and spread its light across the desert that surrounded him, Iron Eyes could see the white-washed sod structures catching the morning rays.

The dark grey mount was lathered up and steaming with exhaustion as the gaunt man galloped into the town. He pulled up outside the crude livery and dismounted. Taking his long rifle out of its leather sheath and untying his saddle bags he banged his fist on the large door until a small Mexican answered. Thrusting a few coins into the man's hand he left the horse in his care.

As he strode along the dusty streets, he watched the sleeping town around him. It was not so much a town as a gathering of white houses. As he headed toward the only word in English he could see he wondered if this was where he would get his man.

The word 'HOTEL' was painted upon the tall, white-washed face of the building. It had almost disappeared after years of bleaching by the cruel sun.

Entering the cool of the building he stopped and paused for a few seconds to allow his eyes to adjust.

Then he saw the small, dark-tanned man with the long moustache hanging from his face. The greased hair had a shine about it that was very strange to Iron Eyes' way of thinking.

'Room,' Iron Eyes said in a tone that was almost demanding.

The small man nodded and handed over a key. There was no way that this man was about to raise any objections to this evil-looking stranger. The steel-cold stare had conveyed its message effectively.

No further words were spoken as the bounty-hunter marched up the stairs.

The small man rushed from the building as if he had to tell someone some very important news.

It was well after eleven that same morning

when the knock upon Iron Eyes' hotel door echoed around the sparse room.

'Come in,' came the growling snarl.

The handle turned cautiously, and the middle-aged man stepped into the bright resting-place. He was a law officer of sorts, by the tin star upon his vest. His white sombrero perched upon the crown of his head denoted a man who had seldom been required to take any action.

Iron Eyes sat upon the top of the bed, still fully dressed and looking like a scarecrow from hell. Even in Rio Drago they had heard of the man.

'You want something?' Iron Eyes questioned.

The smaller man hesitated near the frame of the doorway as if he wished a quick escape route out of this room. His dark eyes hidden under the greying brows studied Iron Eyes who was propped against three pillows. At either side of him, only inches away from his fingers, the Navy Colts waited.

The lawman cleared his throat and forced the words out of his dry mouth. They were not his words, they were the words of concerned citizens.

'Are you Iron Eyes?'

'Could be.'

'If you are, it would please the town elders if you could get your business done very quickly and. . .' There was a long pause before the man finished his sentence. 'Leave.'

Iron Eyes was motionless as he rested his chin

on his chest and watched the man through his black eyebrows.

'You seen a critter named Dan Hardy?'

'Eh, yes,' the man stammered.

Iron Eyes watched the man as sweat began to stream from the brim of his sombrero, down over his dark face.

'He still around?'

'I cannot say.'

As fast as anything the lawman had ever seen, the thin hands had grabbed up the two Navy Colts and brought them both up at arm's length. The grey pupils focused down the barrels at their target. The small man felt his knees shake at the suddenness of the action and the realization of what might follow.

'Try,' Iron Eyes snarled.

'He is in the *cantina*, sir,' the man blurted.

As quickly as he had drawn the two weapons, Iron Eyes replaced them beside him upon the quilted bed cover.

'Thank you.'

The lawman was about to turn to leave when the stranger's voice tore through him.

'Where you going?'

'I was—'

'We ain't finished our confab.' Iron Eyes slithered down the bed and rose above the man's shoulder. 'We gotta continue our talk.'

The smaller man slowly faced his aggressive

14

companion and forced himself to stare up into the dead eyes that burned down at him.

'What else we gotta discuss, sir?'

'We gotta talk about Hardy.' Iron Eyes stretched out his thin arm and pushed the door shut. As it clicked tightly, the lawman felt a cold shiver run along his spine.

'Hardy?'

'Yep.'

'Explain.' The smaller man found himself unable to maintain eye contact with the tall, gaunt figure.

Iron Eyes paced around the man, and the smell of the trail lingered in his wake. It was the aroma of death.

'If you were to leave now, you might high-tail it over to the *cantina* and warn Hardy.'

'I guess he already knows of your presence in Rio Drago.' The man nervously coughed out his words. 'Everyone knows you are in town.'

Iron Eyes' expression changed. It looked like a man who was about to explode in fury as he paced across to his pistols and rammed them into his pants. Then he moved to the chair, plucked up his long dusty coat and pulled it on. The rattling bullets within the pockets sounded like distant spurs.

'Outta my way,' Iron Eyes roared as he strode at the door. Flinging it open he continued down the hall.

Nervously, the small man with the tin star pinned to his vest edged his way out on to the landing and stared down at the charging figure of Iron Eyes as he marched out of the hotel.

THREE

Iron Eyes continued his relentless march up the centre of the deserted street. Dust rose around his feet as he aimed his boots at the *cantina*.

Twenty-three steps later he walked through the hanging beaded curtain and stopped.

The noise of the beads was the only sound within the dark, cool room. A startled bartender was frozen at the sight of the thin killing-machine. Iron Eyes stood like a statue as he absorbed the room. Only his eyes moved as they flashed around the scene before him. One elderly Mexican man sat at a table with a spoon in his hand and a half-eaten bowl of chilli before him. The old man had stopped eating when he had seen Iron Eyes. Now only the flies moved around the brown food.

It seemed like hours but in reality was only a matter of seconds before Iron Eyes heard the noise to his left. The corner was hidden in shadows but the bounty hunter had heard the sound that he had heard many times before. It was the sound of a pistol being pulled from its leather holster.

Iron Eyes did not hesitate.

With a movement that defied belief, he had drawn both his long-barrelled Navy Colts from his pants belt and somehow fired into the blackness of the corner. A shot was returned but went wide and was obviously not aimed. This was a bullet leaving the barrel of a gun being held by a man who was falling.

The noise of the body hitting the floor vibrated around the *cantina* as Iron Eyes returned his left pistol into his pants. The old Mexican and the bartender watched silently as the tall, thin figure walked over to the dark corner. To both men's utter shock Iron Eyes fired another bullet into the stricken body before returning the gun into his belt.

Whether the man who lay on the floor had been only wounded before Iron Eyes finished him off was open to conjecture, all that was certain now was that Dan Hardy was indeed dead.

Grabbing Hardy's shirt collar in his bony hand, Iron Eyes dragged the corpse out of the *cantina* and down the long street.

His destination was the small sod-built building that had the word 'SHERIFF' painted along its frontage.

The small man with the tin star stood shaking

as he watched the figure of Iron Eyes approaching with his trophy. The breeze blew the black, limp hair over the gunman's face, making it impossible to see his expression.

Iron Eyes dropped the body of Dan Hardy at the law officer's feet and returned to his full height.

'You wanna see the wanted poster?' Iron Eyes growled.

The sheriff nodded carefully with his shaking, out-held hand.

After studying it for a few moments, he gulped. 'What do you want me to do, sir?'

Iron Eyes looked around the area for telegraph wires. He finally saw them and pointed.

'Wire for my money,' he advised.

The sheriff nodded silently as Iron Eyes headed back down the dusty, windswept street toward the hotel. Then the small man noticed the blood running freely around his boots from the body with such a surprised expression upon its lifeless face.

The message that greeted Iron Eyes as he read the wire did not sit easily in his guts.

He had to ride to a town named El Paso to get his money. The news angered Iron Eyes greatly as he paced around his hotel room, puffing on his long cigar.

El Paso was across the Rio Grande and in Texas. A long, hard ride, with nothing in-between except Apache.

19

The *cantina* fell silent as the gaunt man sat and ate his meal that evening. The music had stopped when he had entered and would not resume until he left. Iron Eyes chewed his chilli thoughtfully as all around him kept their distance.

It was almost midnight when he mounted his grey and rode away from Rio Drago. The moon was still big enough to light his way as he galloped through the barren landscape.

Iron Eyes would continue to ride his mount as fast as the animal could manage. Day after day and night after night. Stopping only to water and feed the beast, Iron Eyes would not rest until he had the money in his saddle-bags.

El Paso was a town that he had been lucky in. Iron Eyes remembered the time when he was walking down one of its long, aimless streets, littered with saloons and whorehouses, when he saw a face in the crowd.

Not just any old face. A face he had seen on a wanted poster. That was all the reason he required to follow the man. It was a long walk before the man stopped to buy himself some comfort from a five-dollar wench, but that was all the time Iron Eyes had required. He called the man's name, and the guns were drawn and fired blindly.

Smoke filled the scene for several minutes before the bounty-hunter found himself standing over the body of a big, fat, pay-day bounty. That day he walked out of the First National Bank with a saddle-bag filled with ten-thousand-dollars-worth of gold.

Iron Eyes still had the ability to see what others missed. His was the eyesight of a bird of prey.

As long as there was a bounty on the head, he would do anything to kill that face.

This had been his life for over a decade since he found making a living out of hunting animals less than profitable. Turning his talents into hunting men did not bother Iron Eyes. In fact, he found killing men far easier than killing animals.

Men often deserved to be dead and buried.

Iron Eyes was always willing to oblige.

As the sun rose on the third day, Iron Eyes had to rein his mount to a premature stop.

He stood in his stirrups and stared ahead. Dust was rising on a hill ahead of him. For a few minutes, the cold grey eyes gazed at the dust and watched as it moved across his path.

There was only one sort of person Iron Eyes hated more than white folks.

'Apache,' he growled.

FOUR

Without a moment's hesitation, Iron Eyes drove the spurs deeply into the flesh of his grey. The mount leapt across the sagebrush and galloped over the high sierra, with its merciless rider hanging on to the reins.

Iron Eyes was heading due east. The grey soon began to flag with total exhaustion as it climbed the steep ridge which led to a valley of ample cover.

The Apache warriors were not slow to spot the dust rising, and soon the entire hunting party had thrown themselves on to their bareback ponies and were in pursuit.

Thrusting his spurs into the grey was doing little but sending spurts of crimson over Iron Eyes' filthy pants and boots. The rider soon realized that his escape was not going to happen easily with this horse.

He had ridden every ounce of strength and

22

energy out of the poor beast. Iron Eyes pulled the reins up hard and felt the horse's legs buckle beneath him as he slid from the saddle, grabbing his Winchester from the sheath as his boots hit the soft sand.

The horse staggered away, seeking rest and water, as its owner marched up the remaining few yards of the slope.

Even in extreme danger, the ruthless bounty-hunter knew no reason to become overly concerned.

The breeze that swept the top of the dune lifted his long coat allowing it to flap like Old Glory. The matted hair whipped across his whiskerless face as he narrowed his hard, cold eyes to study the scene below him.

Cranking the Winchester, he counted seven Apache heading straight at him upon their ponies.

Ponies.

Iron Eyes gave his horse a glance and knew that if he was truly lucky, he just might get himself one of those ponies. It would mean that he would have to kill all the approaching Indians, but that was nothing.

Men were men. Their colour never concerned his bullets or their aim. These were real men that rode at him. Hunters. Not like the majority of cringing critters that he so often encountered.

When you faced an Apache, you faced a real

man that knew nothing of fear. Fear was for mere mortals.

Iron Eyes decided to use his rifle first. That would allow him to pick off the leading braves. He had to time his killing perfectly.

One shot too early would send the empty mounts racing off in all directions. He had to wait until the young warriors were close enough to strike out at him. They would want him dead and strung up for the buzzards to tear off strips of his flesh.

He knew they would never allow a lone rider to get past them alive. He gritted his stained teeth and started to raise his rifle.

His every action was slow and timed.

The Apache grew closer with every passing second. Now he could see their war paint. These were young bucks out for glory to take back to their elders. A few deer or the scalp of a lone white man would gain them their feathers. They would prove themselves to the tribe.

Iron Eyes drew his Winchester up to his shoulder and focused down the long barrel.

The Indians still came. Now he could hear their war cries getting louder and louder in his ears. Any normal man with blood flowing in his veins would have been frightened.

Very frightened.

Yet this was no normal man.

This was Iron Eyes.

The brave young bucks were so close when he started to fire his repeating rifle they could smell his acrid aroma. One by one they were blown off their ponies.

One by one they died where they fell.

The sheer speed of the wrist-action of Iron Eyes was beyond comprehension to these young men.

As he killed the last warrior, Iron Eyes dropped the rifle and raced forward, grabbing at the pinto stallion as it stumbled in the soft sand.

With strength that came from hell itself, the long thin man wrestled the pony to a standstill.

The crude, grass-rope bridle was screwed so tightly around the stallion's nose, the creature could do little but succumb to Iron Eyes.

Within ten minutes, Iron Eyes had transferred his saddle and bags from the broken shell of his grey on to the new, fresh, Indian pony, and was continuing his journey.

Even before the cold-blooded Iron Eyes had left the scene, the buzzards had gathered over his head, encircling the seven blood-soaked bodies below them.

This was an unexpected feast for the black-feathered carrion, as they swooped lower and lower, sending their chilling screeches echoing through the bleak desert.

None of this bothered the bounty-hunter as he continued his journey to El Paso. He smelled the blood money in his wide nostrils as he drove the pinto on at a speed the poor pony had never previously known.

Iron Eyes rode all the remaining hours of that day and the next before he came across life again. The prairie was still as empty as ever to the rider as he approached the river ahead of him.

Then he saw the swollen Rio Grande rolling before him in its never-ceasing journey.

Even the relentless bounty-hunter had to stop.

The pony almost sounded human as Iron Eyes leapt from the saddle. The relief to the poor sweat-lathered animal was evident, as it staggered to the water's edge and drank the cold liquid.

Iron Eyes stood watching the huge breaking water before him with the look of a man who has just discovered his wife in the bed of his best buddy. Losing a buddy can be hard.

He knew that the high water was not normal for this time of the year and that meant that there were floods upstream.

He sat down on a boulder before pulling out a twisted, thin cigar and raising it to his mouth.

His teeth bit off the end of the smoke before he put it into his mouth and searched for his matches. He struck a long, thin, blue-tipped match with his thumbnail, before sucking it into the brown-leafed Havana.

'Damn,' he muttered as he watched the millions of gallons of water passing him every second. Even he could not overcome nature, although he

26

thought about trying.

You cannot kill a river with a .45 but for a long while as he sucked in the smoke of his cigar he felt like shooting the liquid obstruction.

Shaking his head, he decided to camp here for the night before making up his mind on how to proceed.

The pinto was grained and unsaddled before being tethered to a tree-trunk. Iron Eyes wrapped a blanket around his shoulders and slept as he always slept, with both the deadly grey eyes wide open and a Navy Colt gripped firmly in one of his hands.

FIVE

The morning sun created long shadows from the opposite bank as it traced across the high, orange-coloured hills. The light that glared off the water soon flashed into Iron Eyes' face and awoke him.

For a long while, the bounty-hunter sat motionless watching the pony straining vainly to reach the tempting river-water. Iron Eyes got up on his long thin legs and moved to the horse, who nervously ceased his actions when catching sight of his new master.

The day was young, but the river was still too damn high to cross. The anger that swelled up within the breast of the ghostlike figure was evident in the way he turned and kicked out at the scared stallion.

Iron Eyes hated defeat, and this was defeat in its crudest form. Kicking the dust away as he strolled around the horse, he knew that the river was laughing at him. He could hear the laughter

28

emanating from the breaking water as it continuously flowed past him.

Iron Eyes kneeled down and watched the rolling water as it headed for the Gulf, knowing that he would have to head south along the river's edge until he could find a shallow enough spot to cross.

El Paso was only hours away, but he could not get there and get his bounty money. His reward was sitting in a bank calling out to him as he watched a lot of brown water mocking his every move.

By mid-afternoon, Iron Eyes had ridden at least twenty miles south along the rocky edge of the Rio Grande and knew that he was more than likely in Mexico and not his desired Texas. Yet the river continued to mock him.

The waves were rolling as high as his pony's shoulder as they made their lonesome way along the bank of the big wet.

Every curse-word he had ever learned crept past his dry, thin lips as he rode next to the dangerous breaking waves.

Iron Eyes was becoming conditioned to the fact that he might never reach his destination during this day either as he turned a tight, tree-lined corner. There before him he saw something he had not expected to see.

In all its glory, a single wagon stood unhitched. Four large oxen were tied to a long running rope,

and flames from a campfire rose skyward, sending the smell of bacon into the bounty-hunter's
nostrils.

He normally would have avoided such an obsta-
cle blocking his path, but there was no other way
to pass but by riding straight into this small
encampment.

Iron Eyes paused for a moment as his eagle
vision spied out the scene, trying to detect life at
the site. Whoever was cooking that side of salt-
bacon was nowhere to be seen.

Pulling out his favoured Navy Colt and check-
ing it was fully loaded, Iron Eyes spurred the
pony onward toward the fire, gripping the pistol
in his right hand which he kept hanging at his
side.

The pinto trod carefully over the sharp stones
as all unshod horses do. The man steered the
mount closer and closer to the wagon, until he
saw a sight which he had not expected.

It was a woman.

She was tall and thin for a female in these
parts.

The rifle she aimed at him from the cover of the
wagon was cocked and ready. For the first time in
his life, Iron Eyes had ridden himself into a situation that confused him.

He pulled the reins gently and tried not to focus
on the young figure, who was dressed in jeans and
shirt below him.

The sun glinted off the long rifle barrel and danced over his cold, deathlike features.

'Christ, you sure are ugly,' the woman exclaimed aloud.

'You ain't no oil painting yourself.'

Iron Eyes turned his head slowly and glared down at her with the grey pupils burning in anger.

'Howdy, ma'am,' he sneered through his discoloured teeth at her. His tone was sharp, and oozing deadly intent.

'What d'you want?' she snapped.

'A way to get across this river.' He gestured at the furious waves that thundered past the tail-gate of her wagon.

Her shadow was almost as long as his as she paced around the man who was like a statue upon his horse. She noticed the pistol in his hand and stopped. Raising the rifle level with his face she smiled.

It was a smile that was as cold as his own.

'Drop the shooting-iron, mister,' she demanded. 'Or I'll part your hair for you.'

'What?' he growled.

The rifle-shot that nicked the edge of his left ear sent agonizing pain racing through him. A pain that he had never experienced before. The blood gushed from the small wound and dripped over his dark, dirty coat-collar.

'Drop that gun, mister, or the next shot will

31

part your hair between your eyes.' She had cranked the rifle swiftly and expertly.

With satisfaction, she watched the man allow his Navy Colt to drop into the dust at her feet.

'You crazy?' Iron Eyes screamed at her.

'Yep.'

SIX

The two men that rode into Rio Drago were the sort of people every law-respecting person dreads to see arriving. Their horses showed the signs of hard riding as they plodded heavy-footed down the wide, sun-baked street. People scattered at the sight of the two riders.

They surveyed the scene with an amusement born out of years of killing and bank robberies. They had arrived on time as instructed.

Both men knew that this was a place that no smart person would ever visit and that made it perfect. They had been told to meet their brother here. They were low on cash and when his wire had arrived back in Laramie, they took the opportunity to skip out and ride. This had been a place where they always came to meet up with Dan.

Tom and Whit Hardy were younger than their sibling by many years, and knew little about anything apart from doing as he instructed. They were just the hired help of a very clever man, even if they were kin.

Tom Hardy had always been the second man behind Dan. He could not shoot as well as his elder brother, but knew how to scare folks into listening to the older man. He was back-up for the older, wiser, more skilled robber. Tom knew his place. His place was right behind Dan Hardy.

Whit Hardy was young underneath all his whiskers. Young, and very drunk. Drunkenness was his natural state and had been for over five years. When he was drunk he could not remember to be scared, and he was always scared. His was the lowest rung on the Hardy ladder, and all he wanted from life was money, women and liquor. Not necessarily in that order.

Whenever they went into action he drank more and more until he reached a state that folks seldom ever reached without falling down. Whit had become a shadow of his former self, and the yellowing of his teeth was matched by the pupils of his eyes. No man could drink as much as he consumed without shooting holes in their liver. Whit was a young man on the brink of death, and quite happy to continue heading in that downward spiral.

Drinking one's self to death was a darn sight better way to go than the alternative. Whit was the man who stood in the street outside the banks that his elder brothers were robbing. His job was to hold the horses and shoot up the town, making sure that people ran away before his brothers came out with the loot.

Not the most demanding of jobs, but when you are of a nervous nature, and pickled in alcohol, it takes every ounce of energy to do that simple task. Whit Hardy knew his place.

The two riders drew their mounts up outside the *cantina* and dismounted. They tied the horses up firmly to the dried wooden poles that fronted the trough, before entering the place that rang out with the sounds of Mexican music.

They were caked in the dust and grime that only days on such fiery terrain as that which led to Rio Drago could bake on to visitors.

'I'm as dry as hell, Tom,' Whit gasped as he stepped up on to the creaking boardwalk.

'And you needs a drink,' the elder man said.

'That's about it, I guess,' Whit coughed, as they pushed their way in through the beaded curtain.

It was dark inside this place. Dark and cool. A welcome relief from the exterior that seemed to burn under the blazing noon sun.

As they walked to the bartender they watched as the few regulars seemed to cast their eyes away from them. It was obvious that something was wrong. Very wrong indeed.

'Got any whiskey?' Tom asked as they leaned on to the filthy bar.

'We only got tequila,' the bartender said, in a very quiet tone.

35

'Two bottles of that then,' Whit gushed as he fumbled for a few coins in his pocket.

Tom Hardy said nothing as he watched the man behind the bar get two of the bottles off the makeshift shelf behind him. The elder of the brothers turned to study the people who were sitting behind them, when his eyes caught sight of the blood-stained walls in the far corner. Tapping Whit's arm he strolled across the *cantina*, past the guitarist who was trying to earn a few cents, up to the dark corner.

Tom Hardy's eyes travelled over the scene of the bullets and blood that confronted him.

It was no normal sight, even for his tired eyes.

'That weren't there last time we was here, Tom,' Whit drawled as he touched the holes in the wall. 'Looks fresh to me.'

Tom turned and retraced his steps back to the bar. He was still silent as he poured himself a tall glass of the clear liquor and downed it in one. Then he repeated the action, before looking up at the timid man bahind the bar.

'Who did that?'

'A man. An evil man. *Gringo* like you,' the stammering bartender replied.

'Name?' Tom snapped.

'He called Iron Eyes, I think.'

Whit grabbed his brother's sleeve. 'The bounty-hunter.'

'Yep. The stinking gut-slime bounty-hunter.'

36

Tom swallowed another drink.

'Who did he kill?' Whit swigged from his bottle.

The man behind the bar went suddenly very pale as he trembled before them. 'I am afraid it was your brother Dan, *amigo*.'

'Dan?' Tom went weak at his knees as he spoke his brother's name.

'Not Dan,' Whit dribbled in disbelief. 'Nobody was as fast as Dan. Nobody at all.'

'This varmint called Iron Eyes was very fast.' The barman shook his head in sorrow at the loss of such a good patron.

Tom Hardy poured himself another drink in an attempt to try and calm himself down. He swallowed the drink and rubbed his wet mouth with his dirty sleeve before managing to speak once again.

'Where is this Iron Eyes?'

'I think he left town,' the bartender replied.

'With my brother's body?'

'No. He went alone.'

Tom led the way out of the *cantina*, with his brother close behind, and headed for the small white building with the word 'SHERIFF' painted upon its frontage.

'What we doing?' Whit asked as he walked, holding on to his bottle tightly.

'Going to see the sheriff,' Tom replied.

'What for?'

Tom Hardy did not answer as he strode angrily

across the wide open space between the *cantina* and the small home of the law. His feet were suddenly filled with a strength that only anger can muster.

The door of the sheriff's office flew open as the elder Hardy brother marched in and scared the life out of the small man with the star pinned to his chest.

Before the shaking man could rise from his chair behind the brittle desk, the hands of Tom Hardy had dragged him up into the air.

'Where is the body of my brother Dan?' he screamed at the man he was holding.

'Over in the undertaker's. Across the street,' came the reply that vibrated with every shake forced into it.

Tom Hardy released his grip and watched as the man fell to his knees.

'And Iron Eyes?' he shouted.

The smaller man clambered up on to his legs and shook with terror before answering. 'He had to go to El Paso to collect his reward money.'

'Reward money? Blood money, you mean,' Tom snapped as he stood breathing hard.

'*Si, amigo*. Blood money,' the man agreed. 'I could not stop him. He was evil. Possessed.'

Whit Hardy grabbed at his brother's sleeve.

'What the hell do you want, boy?' Tom shouted.

'Let's go.'

'Where?'

'Any place,' Whit swigged at his bottle, 'away from here.'

'You scared?' Tom looked at his brother's face hard and long, watching the sweat pouring down from under his Stetson.

'You bet I'm scared,' Whit nodded.

'I ain't. I'm angry. Angrier than hell.' Tom Hardy looked at the lawman again. 'When did this Iron Eyes lit out?'

'Some days ago, *amigo*.'

Tom strode out of the small building and across the street, with his brother at his heels once more.

'What're you thinking, Tom?'

Tom opened the door and walked into the dark, shadowy place, coming to a sudden halt at the sight before him. Whit bumped into his back as they were confronted by the true horror of the situation.

Lying naked to the waist on a slab of stone lay what was left of Dan Hardy. It was a vision of what their profession held for them both in the near future. The bullet holes had been washed clean, but the sight was still more than either man had expected when they had walked into this gloomy place.

Tom was the first to leave the building, and he found the edge of a water-trough comfort for his backside. He sat there for many minutes as his younger sibling threw up the contents of his guts into the sand at the side of the white-washed building.

Vengeance is mine, the Lord said in the good book.

Tom Hardy forced himself upright once more with those words and thoughts filling his mind. He would not wait for God to catch up with Iron Eyes, he had to do this himself.

Whit finally quit being sick and staggered to the side of his brother, who had the strangest look in his eyes.

'What're you thinking, Tom?'

'We are gonna do some hunting, boy,' Tom growled.

'What?'

'We are gonna hunt that Iron Eyes varmint down and kill him for what he done to Dan.' Tom Hardy started to walk again.

'Don't start going crazy, Tom,' Whit pleaded as he tried to keep pace.

'Crazy?' Tom grunted. 'It ain't crazy to avenge a wrong, is it?'

Whit followed his brother into the cool *cantina* once again, and knew that he had more good reasons to get himself well oiled. If they were going to start tracking the man who was known throughout the West as the living ghost, he had better be real drunk in case they caught up with the critter.

Iron Eyes took no prisoners.

'Dead or alive' meant dead to the bounty-hunter.

Even through the haze of liquor that permanently blurred his thoughts, Whit knew they were heading into the lion's mouth head-first by going after him.

Even Whit knew that.

So how come Tom was so darned eager to chase this killer of men and collector of rewards?

Could he want to die so badly that he would risk everything by pursuing the man in the long coat?

As they prepared to eat another bowl of chilli and biscuits as hard as stones, Whit knew that he had to stick with his brother and hope the fire would leave him before it was too late. Dan was gone, and so were their futures. Without Dan they would find it hard to rob old ladies, let alone banks.

Times were changing for the Hardys.

Whit and Tom Hardy were like two grizzly bears as they saddled up their reliable mounts. They had sore heads and sore butts. The silence was overwhelming as the two remaining Hardy brothers gathered up their few belongings into the faded leather saddle-bags.

The two men had ridden into Rio Drago the previous afternoon, only to find their elder brother laid out upon a slab in the back of the undertaker's office.

Even after laying the few reasonable town whores and drinking their fill of the locally distilled tequila, they were still angry. They had spent almost all their money since their last job and had joined their brother to plan another. Not that they could plan anything themselves. It had always been Dan who had made all the decisions.

Dan knew how to stage a hold-up.

Dan knew from which side to enter each town, and which was the quickest route to safety after they had done their deed. Now Dan was lying upon a slab, and his only use was to allow the numerous varieties of flies to lay their eggs upon his rotting carcass.

The drink had made the pair even more angry than they originally were upon discovering Dan's death.

Now they had hangovers which matched their moods.

The throbbing of the blood as it tried to penetrate their brains was like drums as it echoed around their skulls.

Pain had driven the two men into making the decision to find and kill Iron Eyes.

Not the pain of grief but the pain of self-infliction.

Revenge brooded in both men's hearts as they managed to absorb the simple fact that Iron Eyes had blown their brother away for the bounty upon his unwashed head.

Having an instinctive dislike for men who made their living out of blood money, the two

Hardys decided to try and catch up with the lone gunman before he reached El Paso.

It might not have been a perfect plan, as Tom and Whit were also wanted for exactly the same reasons as their late sibling, but brains never had been their strong point.

They were going to chase and catch Iron Eyes.

They were also going to shoot and kill the son of a bitch.

Neither man had half a brain between them, and had followed Dan's lead all their lives. He said draw your guns and they drew their guns. Dan said shoot up the town and they shot up the town.

Now Dan Hardy was being prepared for burial.

Now his mind was gone and they would have to fend for themselves as well as they could.

The black clouds that drifted over Rio Drago started to unleash rain that made the cactus sing, and the two weathered men finished their task. The horses were ready.

Heading inside the small *cantina* that still had the stains of their brother's blood on its whitewashed walls, the two men purchased their supplies.

Three bottles of tequila and a bag of salt each would have to do until they reached a town that sold rotgut rye. The two bowls of chilli and kilnbaked bread filled their bellies long enough for them to get back to their horses.

43

'Where we headed?' Whit asked, finishing his bread as he pulled himself up into the saddle by the saddle-horn.

Tom Hardy dragged himself up into his own saddle, after forcing the tequila bottles into his saddle-bags. His frustration showed as he gathered up the loose reins and pulled the horse away from the rail.

'We are after the creep who killed our brother, Whit,' he snarled, spitting the remnants of animal bone from between his sparse teeth. 'Remember?'

Whit shrugged and took a long swig from his bottle, shaking his head violently as the strong liquor reached his brain. The journey did not take long.

'We are after Iron Eyes,' Whit grinned as he allowed his nag to turn away from the hitching-rail and join his awaiting brother.

'Right,' Tom agreed as he twisted his neck in order to relieve the pain that still hammered inside his head. No matter how hard he tried, the combination of cheap liquor and rotten grub took its toll upon his demeanour. He felt like hell and he was angry.

The gormless Whit sat as he dribbled the burning tequila from his dry lips.

'That's right. Ain't it, Tom?' he gushed. 'I is right, ain't I?'

Tom Hardy nodded and then shook his head in frustration at his dim-witted brother, not that he was ever going to be mistaken for a genius himself.

The two riders rode out of the small Latin township and faithfully followed the route that the feeble law officer had pointed out.

They had revenge in their hearts but little else. These were two men who would try and catch up with the man who was heading to El Paso to collect his blood money.

What neither man knew was that the man they chased was the most evil and dangerous man they could ever hope to meet. Not that any normal man would wish to catch up with Iron Eyes and his pair of Navy Colts.

The two remaining Hardy brothers were neither normal nor were they too smart. They were the body of the chicken after the axe had removed the head of the bird. They were the two lesser Hardy brothers and their brain had been removed.

Dan Hardy was dead.

Whit and Tom Hardy were heading after his executioner with plenty of liquor in not only their saddle-bags but their guts too.

They would chase their brother's killer for no better reason than they were going to make him pay.

As the dust rose behind their horses' hooves, the remaining hours of their futile lives were beginning to run out. Like sand through a pail with a hole in its bottom, the end was getting closer with every stride their mounts took.

Smarter men would have reasoned the odds and quit their riding after a known killer like Iron Eyes. The trouble with dumb folks is that they follow the beats of their hearts, rather than the messages from their heads, because the messages in their brains usually are not worth listening to.

They were heading toward hell.

There would be no prisoners taken.

Only death would end this quest for revenge.

Unfortunately, death had ridden on Iron Eyes' shoulder for many a long while.

SEVEN

It was late afternoon before the rifle-woman allowed the gaunt Iron Eyes to dismount from his Indian pony.

The sun was setting below the far-away hills that marked the Texas side of the wide river.

It was still unbelievably hot, and the sweat had soaked through both their shirts. Now every detail of her fine-formed breasts could be seen by the sharp-eyed bounty-hunter.

He had continued bleeding from the hole in his ear for over an hour, and his shoulder was stained with his own blood.

She watched as he bent down to pick up the tin plate she had indicated. He helped himself to a slice of burned bacon and sat down upon the hard ground. It tasted good, he thought, as he chewed the meat and watched her with squinting eyes.

Whoever she was, she was good.

She had done something no other living person had ever managed to do. She had taken a chunk out of him.

Iron Eyes respected her for the attitude she displayed toward him. It was like his own. Merciless.

She walked around him and never once allowed the long rifle barrel to wander off its chosen target, his head.

'Who're you chasing?' she asked as she finally stopped pacing through the soft sand.

'Nobody,' he replied, with the black-and-pink meat sticking to his uneven teeth.

'You look like a hunter of men,' she said, sitting down on a large boulder opposite him.

'I am.'

'So who're you after?'

'Nobody at the moment.' He pushed the remaining lump of bacon into his mouth and chewed. It was the first solid food he had eaten for several days, apart from hard tack.

'So you're a bounty-hunter?' She reached down and picked up the black tin mug full of coffee. 'That is an evil trade.'

'Suits my character,' he sneered, picking his teeth with his fingernails.

'You good at it?'

'The best there ever was,' he bragged.

'You are the best?' She gave a belly laugh. 'How come I got the drop on you then?'

He shrugged. It was a shrug that disguised his anger.

'You got lucky.'

'No, my friend.' She sipped her coffee. 'You got lucky.'

'Me?'

'I didn't kill you. That's damn lucky.'

He nodded as he dropped the plate on to the sand. His mood was changing. He was no longer angry at having a chunk of his ear blown away. Now he wanted to know more about this woman who sat before him.

'What do they call you?' he asked.

'What does it matter?'

'I like to know who the hell shoots me.' Iron Eyes felt the stinging ease up on the side of his head. The blood was finally clotting on his wound.

'They call me Jane.' She tossed the sentence away like a child would toss away its favourite rag-doll. Her eyes looked at him with the look of a woman who was interested in something she had captured. His long coat and hair were not what she had become used to seeing in the past few years of her life. He looked as if he were the sort of man who held up trains in dime novels. Her curiosity about this painfully thin man was the only reason she had not killed him.

For some reason she wanted to know more about this creature, who looked as if he belonged in some graveyard rather than out here upon the plains.

'Jane what?'

'Jane is enough,' she growled.

He accepted that he was not getting any further with that line of questioning, and decided to alter his approach.

'Where you headed?'

'West.'

'What the hell do you wanna go there for?' he asked, as he cautiously touched the scab upon his ear. 'There ain't nothing in that direction except Indians and Mexicans.'

'Suits me.' She finished her coffee and got to her feet.

Iron Eyes rose to his full height, which was only barely taller than her. He studied her body. She was thinner than any woman he had ever seen. She was also the first female he had ever seen wearing men's clothes. He liked what he was looking at.

'What you thinking?' She glared at him, with the rifle still balanced in her hands.

'Nothing.' He blew out heavily, trying to clear his brain of the thoughts that had raced through him. Thoughts that sent the skin on his thin neck tingling. She had a body that he would gladly kill for. That was strange for Iron Eyes, as he had never once before been tempted by a female. She was somehow different.

Very different.

'What do they call you, Mr Bounty-hunter?'

'Iron Eyes,' he drawled. 'Just Iron Eyes.'

For the first time since they had run into each other, her face went pale, as if suddenly shocked.

The name meant something to her, but what?

She looked him up and down carefully for what seemed an eternity, before lowering the rifle.

'Iron Eyes?' She repeated his words.

'Yep.' He felt very uneasy by this creature and her sudden mood-swing. The hostility had vanished.

Yet it had been replaced by something totally alien to this ruthless man's knowledge.

'I heard about you.' Her eyes darted at him briefly, before turning away once more.

'Anything good?'

'Depends on your point of view.'

Iron Eyes looked at the lowered rifle, and then stepped closer to the slim lady with the emotion-less face.

'You ain't aiming that iron at me any more,' he said, resting his knuckles upon his bony hips.

She nodded and moved away from him. She seemed deep in thought as she paced through the soft sand.

Finally, she stopped, and turned her attention to the raging waters of the swollen river as it roared past them with an unceasing fury.

'Yesterday that river was about six inches deep.'

Iron Eyes closed in on her.

'That when you crossed?'

'Yeah, that's when I crossed,' she replied.

She could feel his breath upon her neck as he stopped at her side and hovered, like a bee watching a flower. Ready to take the pollen. Finally she turned and gazed into his cold eyes.

'What you looking at?'

Iron Eyes did not answer. He just continued staring at her, with hunger in his face. The hunger of a man who had never before seen something that whetted his appetite.

EIGHT

Dawn came silently, and a new day arrived with the usual burning sun and blinding light. Somehow the tall, thin man with the two Navy Colts tucked into his pants belt had managed to sleep for several hours.

Iron Eyes had stayed near the wagon into which she had climbed the previous evening, but never once moved closer.

Jane had worried him.

She had confused him.

She had shot a chunk of his left ear off and lived to tell the tale.

Now he stood watching the raging waters rolling past their campsite, wondering what he should do next. All thoughts of just saddling up his pony and riding away had left his mind. He kept casting a silent glance at the wagon, wondering when she would step out into the morning sunshine.

The money he was owed in El Paso no longer

seemed important to the hard man. Yet he could not understand why. His thin fingers touched the edge of his ear, and he winced at the stinging pain that met him as he found the scabbed wound.

A woman had blown a piece of his ear off and she still lived and breathed. He accepted the fact.

Iron Eyes had once shot the head off a man for bumping into him in a saloon and causing him to spill his beer. He knelt down and cupped the fresh water in his hands, and tossed it over his face and head. This was not an action that was based upon wishing to become clean but a desire to try and wake up.

He stood once more as the water ran down his hair and face on to his shirt. He rubbed his smooth chin and wondered why he had never had a growth of whiskers like other menfolk. He felt that he must have been part Indian never to have developed hair on his narrow face. Having only a scant recall of his mother and absolutely no knowledge of who his father might have been, it was a distinct possibility.

He dragged his long legs through the sand to the pony who had remained tied to a wheel of the wagon all night. He looked at the pinto and then the large nearby oxen.

How did a girl manage to handle such a team?

Horses were tough enough, but the oxen were monsters in comparison to even the largest horses he had ever encountered.

Where was she heading or where was she running from?

He checked his two Navy Colts and then put them back into his belt, before wondering why he was hanging around this place with this strange woman.

If the river's level had dropped during the night, he might have saddled the pony and ridden away. He might have, but even he doubted it.

This female named Jane had made him curious enough to alter his plans, if only briefly.

He kept thinking of the reward money, waiting for him across the wide Rio Grande, and how he would normally not let anything slow his progress at collecting it. Yet, for the first time in many years, he felt as if there was no hurry.

The money would still be there even if he took another couple of days to reach El Paso. He had killed his way across many territories and was tired of all the blood.

It was time to let the blood on his hands dry before killing any more.

Iron Eyes turned and watched as the canvas flap was opened and a long, blue-denim-clad leg poked out. The rest of Jane's slim body followed, and she came to ground next to the dripping bounty-hunter, in her hands a towel and some feminine objects like a brush and soap.

'Morning,' she said in her usual one-tone voice.

He acknowledged her with a slight movement of his head, and then continued to tend to his pinto.

'You fall in the river?' she asked, with something that might have been regarded as a smile upon any other female's face but hers.

'What's your meaning?' he asked.

Her hand touched his dripping hair.

Iron Eyes shrugged, and leaned over to his saddle-bags. He emptied some oats on to the sand, and watched as the pony started to consume them quickly, before aiming his gaze at her.

'Where you heading?' There was an innocence in his question that ill suited him.

'A gal gotta do what a gal gotta do,' she snapped as she headed down to the water's edge.

Iron Eyes watched her as she did what she had to do. She never once tried to hide herself away from his burning eyes. She seemed either unaware of his watching or cared little for his attention.

Iron Eyes wanted her.

Like a dog wants a bitch.

There was nothing romantic in his feelings. He was not sweet on her. He was no female-starved cowboy hitting town with only one thought on his mind. He wanted her for reasons that were totally alien to him.

Without any feelings of guilt, he kept watching her as she did what she had to do. His face strained at the sight of something that he had never before witnessed.

The tall bounty-hunter found it a magnetic draw for his hard eyes.

Rubbing his neck, he finally turned away, long after he should have done so. Strangely, she seemed to have no concern about his watching her every action.

It was as if she were trying to tempt him into acting like a man with blood flowing through his veins rather than staining his clothes and boots.

It was a chance that was even slimmer than his starved body.

She pulled up her britches, and then returned back to the long, dark figure in the long, dark coat. Although he held his chin on his chest and his long wet hair covered his face, she could see his every expression written in his every sinew.

As she brushed past him, the aroma of soap filled his nostrils and made him look up as she tossed the towel and things into the back of the wagon once more.

Iron Eyes grabbed at her slim arm and breathed heavily as he looked at her eyes which were staring back at him. The mutual mind-reading lasted several seconds before he felt his grip loosen.

'What?' she asked.

Iron Eyes released his grip and her arm fell from his fingers to her side. He gritted his teeth and grunted in a confused state, before rubbing his nose with his sleeve.

'Nothing,' he muttered.

'You still figuring on heading for El Paso?' she asked firmly.

'Yep,' he replied, feeling as if he had just lost a fight that he did not know he had been involved in. 'Guess so.'

She pointed at the still-rolling waves that were lashing even more furiously than the previous day.

'You got a long ride south then, Mr Iron Eyes.'

'How far south?' He placed his attention on the raging river and focused his keen eyes.

'A long ways south.' The female seemed to know a lot more about the Rio Grande than her bounty-hunting companion. 'Maybe a hundred miles before this swell widens out to a point where we can get across.'

'A hundred miles?' Iron Eyes felt like shooting the damn river again just for being there. 'A hundred miles? You're sure of that?'

'Nope.' She spat at the ground. 'But it's a fair guess.'

Iron Eyes rubbed the back of his filthy neck and just growled at the thought of his money sitting in El Paso and him stuck on the wrong side of the widest, wildest river in hell. The sun burned down on them as they faced each other.

'You wanted to join me last night, didn't you?'

she said in a blunt tone.

He seemed to agree without opening his mouth.

'Then why didn't you?' Her question hit him hard between his cold, steel-coloured eyes.

'You already shot off one of my ears for doing nothing.' He answered quietly. 'I wasn't gonna risk you shooting off anything valuable.'

She heaved her chest up and kept him firmly fixed in her sights.

'That was before I knew who you was.'

'What difference does that make?' Iron Eyes' face had a sudden look of curiosity etched across it.

There was no answer to his question, just the glimmer of a hint that he might not have been rejected as quickly as he had assumed.

'Where you heading with this rig?' Iron Eyes tried to change the subject that he was clearly finding hard to resolve.

Jane was silent for the longest time before answering the bounty-hunter.

'South?' For the first time she witnessed what could only be described as a faint smile cross his lips as he sucked her words into his soul.

'You figure on joining me on my trip, Jane?' He somehow managed to spit his words out.

She grabbed a pan off its hook on the side of the wagon, and headed for the ashes of her campfire. He watched her every step with an interest that was unusual for him. Kneeling down, she placed the pan on to the sand before gazing up at his face.

'If you get some kindling I'll fix us some grub.'

Iron Eyes gazed down at her, and found himself obeying her orders willingly.

NINE

The two remaining Hardy brothers had ridden long and hard before they spied the buzzards circling above the far-off mesa. It was the more observant Tom who reined his mount to a halt first and stood high in his stirrups.

The sight ahead bothered him greatly, and, for the first time since setting out from Rio Drago, he was concerned at what might lie ahead for them.

The dark clouds did little to help him as he pulled up the high collar of his over-jacket to shield his ears from the chilling breeze.

Death lay over the far off ridge, and his guts ached at the thought that revenge might not be such an easy task. He and his drunken brother had to try and catch the bounty-hunter named Iron Eyes before he crossed the Rio Grande and headed into the far more populous Texas to get his blood money. It was a task that had soured in Tom's mouth for the past few hours as the constant riding had sobered him up.

The slower Whit Hardy pulled up to a halt beside his brother, and sat spitting out the flies from his teeth. Swaying in his saddle he could barely focus on his horse's mane, let alone the far-off mesa which seemed to be occupying his brother's attention. To Whit the only thought had been to have another drink of his powerful Mexican brew.

It was nowhere near as tasty as whiskey, but it served its purpose and kept the reality of their situation at a distance.

'You see that, Whit?' Tom balanced himself by holding on to the reins as he hovered in his stirrups.

Whit looked at his brother and then at the distant birds that circled in the far-away sky. Removing his Stetson and scratching his lice-infested head, he tried to work out what the fuss was all about.

'I see a bunch of crows or something. So what?' he drawled in his usual manner. The sight was hardly enough to get him worked up into a lather.

Tom sat back down in his saddle and glared at the man beside him. The expression was one of total frustration.

'Them's buzzards, Whit,' he sighed.

'So?' The younger man reached back into his saddle-bag and withdrew a bottle. Finding it empty he tossed it away and fished out another.

This one was full to the cork, which he pulled with his teeth.

'Buzzards flying around in a circle?' Tom tried to get a response from his tequila-swigging sibling. 'Think about it, boy.'

Whit pulled the bottle from his lips and gave a yell of sudden awareness.

'Something is dead over there,' Whit ranted, with an excitement in his voice that was as rare as finding him without glazed eyes.

Tom blew long and hard and prodded his horse with his sharp spurs. The mount started to move ahead at a slow pace. He was headed for the mesa and the buzzards.

The younger man followed with reins in one hand and the bottle in the other. He had long forgotten why they were on this journey, and the constant consumption of homemade liquor seemed to keep his brain permanently blurred.

Whit Hardy followed his brother up over the sand dunes until they reached the level top which rolled down on to the almost flat prairie.

Tom sat, leaning on his saddle-horn, glaring at the sight before him. It was totally horrific and at first very difficult to make out, but gradually both riders knew what they had ridden in on.

This was a sight seldom seen.

This was the remnants of a one-sided battle that the shredded bodies before them were testament to.

This was the work of Iron Eyes.

The bodies of the Apache warriors were scattered around, and had been plucked almost free of flesh since they had been slaughtered. The buzzards that circled were waiting their turn at the feast below, as other birds ripped at the rotting flesh. A handful of ponies were away in the distance, having remained close to their fallen masters.

Whit lowered his bottle to his side and turned to throw up. He chucked his guts up into the hot dry sand.

The smell was like nothing either man had ever experienced in all their days.

Even the more battle-scarred Tom felt the bitter taste of vomit in his mouth as he inhaled the terrible stench.

'Indians,' Tom managed to say. 'Them bodies used to be Indians, boy.'

Whit continued being sick as the mixture of acrid aroma and cheap liquor filled him.

Soon the two men had left the carnage behind them as they followed the trail left by the unshod pony. The bodies might have been getting more distant behind their horses as they proceeded ahead, but the smell lingered in the two riders' noses. No matter how hard they rode, they could not get the stink out of their heads.

With gritted teeth, Tom Hardy leaned over his saddle-horn and rode toward the far-off golden hills, leading his swaying brother behind him.

Whoever this man named Iron Eyes was, he was sure good with his guns, the outlaw thought.

The sweat ran down his spine beneath his thick shirt.

It was not the sweat of a man suffering from excess heat, but the sweat of a man who was scared of what lay ahead. The trail was easy to follow. It was like the bounty-hunter himself, straight to the point.

The ghosts of his many victims seemed to be howling in the chilling wind. They were being urged on by all the notches upon the guns of Iron Eyes.

Tom Hardy was no gunslinger, he was always the man who followed his daring brother Dan into the banks. He was better than the dim-witted Whit, yet that was nothing to write home about. After his usual intake of booze, Whit could be outdrawn by his horse.

Tom knew that chasing the deadly Iron Eyes was foolhardy, but continued heading after the bounty hunter anyway.

Who the hell was this varmint called Iron Eyes? It was a question that would ride inside Tom Hardy's head for the rest of their journey.

He had little else to think about as the cold breeze blew at their spines and chewed into their bones.

Who was this Iron Eyes?

TEN

The thin, ghostlike figure of Iron Eyes sat upon his pinto, holding the reins tightly in his left hand, as he watched the three mounted riders approaching from the south.

The mysterious Jane had pulled her wagon to a standstill behind the bounty hunter, and looped the reins around the long brake-pole at her side. She had automatically lifted her Winchester out of the box at her feet and cranked it ready for action. She sat on the wooden plank with her foot resting on the brake as she studied the riders over her oxen and the statuesque Iron Eyes.

The large sombreros gave the clue as to where these men were from, but not who or what they were. It was known that bandits were commonplace in the more remote regions of the prairie, but these might be ranchers.

The river flowed to their left-hand side as both Iron Eyes and Jane sat watching the riders.

They had travelled over ten miles along the edge of the wild river, trying to find a suitable place to attempt a crossing.

Iron Eyes sat watching the three men as they grew ever closer, without changing his expression. His grey pupils were like two musket-balls as they focused upon the men. He had heard the rifle being cocked for action behind him, and knew that the strange female was ready to blow off a few more ears if not worse.

His fingers stroked the pistol tucked over his left hip as they started to pull their horses up. All three men were skilled riders by the way they stopped their headstrong stallions. These were not the sort of horses that just anyone could ride. These were strong, rampant steeds that only masters of their trade could hope to handle.

Each man sat below his vast sombrero, watching the ghostlike figure and the female on top of the wagon. They were dressed in a fashion that was almost artistic in its detail. All were clad in black, with white-and-silver patterns. Their frilly white shirts and red scarves seemed to highlight their obvious vanity.

'Well?' Iron Eyes growled in a slow manner that seemed to question the riders' right to be before him.

The one rider who seemed to have an understanding of English removed his large sombrero and made a flowing gesture with it as he smiled.

His hair gleamed in the sunshine from expensive oils as he replaced it on to his head.

'I am Dwan José Valdez, *señor*,' he informed in a tone that seemed to warrant applause. 'Welcome to my humble *rancho*.'

Iron Eyes gave a backward glance at the female who sat with the Winchester across her lap, before returning his attention to the trio of men.

'You own this strip of land?' Iron Eyes asked.

The man who had given his name raised both shoulders and made a curious expression that was partly masked by his long, waxed moustache.

'Not this exact spot but everything else over here.' He waved his left arm and pointed away from the wide, rolling river.

'What do you want of us?' Iron Eyes continued to thumb the Navy Colt as he spoke to the riders.

The man called Valdez continued to smile at the dark, narrow-eyed bounty-hunter as his two outriders sat nervously looking silently on. They too kept their hands upon the hammers of their pistols.

'I am here to ask why you have entered our lands.'

'Just heading south,' Iron Eyes muttered under his breath, as he lowered his chin until it rested upon his chest. 'Trying to find a safe place to cross this angry river.'

'But south is no good.' Valdez smiled in a manner that was beginning to make the gaunt man angry.

'Why not?'

'I own all the land south from here,' Valdez gestured. 'I cannot allow people to cross my land uninvited.'

'You own the river?' Iron Eyes turned as he heard Jane ask her simple, blunt question. He found yet another smile starting to cross his lips.

Valdez gazed up at the woman in surprise.

'No, dear lady. I do not own the river but—' he admitted.

'Quit holding us up and get your fancy back-sides out of our way,' Jane shouted in a way that made all three Mexican riders uneasy.

'You misunderstand me, dear lady.' Valdez regained his composure and his smile as he aimed his conversation at the woman with the rifle.

'How so?' she asked.

'I wish you to be my guests at my *rancho*.' Valdez bowed as he spoke to her. 'It is our custom.'

Jane was very unimpressed. 'You often invite strangers to your home?'

'We seldom see strangers.' Valdez was feeling uneasy at the way the dark, long-haired Iron Eyes toyed with the handle of his pistol. 'We cannot allow you to continue your journey without offering our simple home for you to rest and refresh yourselves.'

'Why not?' Iron Eyes grunted.

'You are not of these parts. It is our custom.' Dwan José Valdez had imparted a tone into his explanation that seemed to suggest that he would never accept any refusals.

Iron Eyes pulled hard on his reins and forced the pony to step backward until it was level with the wagon. The thin man looked up at Jane. His eyes were as glassy as ever, but he seemed to be urging her to accept the invitation.

'We better take up the offer,' he advised.

'Why?' Jane seemed ready to blow holes in the bunch of smartly dressed *vaqueros*. 'I ain't afraid of no dandies.'

'I am,' Iron Eyes found himself honestly admitting. 'I learned a long time ago never to underestimate your opponents. It can be costly.'

'You scared?' She seemed shocked that he was unwilling to engage in a shoot-out.

'Nope. I just do not want to get ventilated before I get to El Paso and collect my reward money.' He spat at the sand as he studied the Mexicans.

'Are you sure?'

'I reckon they might not take kindly to our refusing.' Iron Eyes pulled a cigar from inside his coat and pushed it between his uneven teeth.

'You sure you ain't scared, Iron Eyes?' Jane kept watching the three men as she spoke to her companion.

Iron Eyes gave a brief laugh before answering her. 'I seen these sort of varmints before. They get kinda upset if you refuse their hospitality.'

'How upset?' She was curious.

'The Mexicans around here are part Indian. They got strange ideas on manners.' Iron Eyes struck a match and inhaled the welcome smoke.

Jane was still confused, but decided to go along with Iron Eyes' advice.

'You better be right,' she snarled, grabbing the cigar from out of Iron Eyes' mouth and ramming it into her own.

Iron Eyes sank his spurs into the pinto's flesh and rode forward to the three strange men.

'Thanks,' he said quietly. 'We accept your most kind and generous offer, Valdez.'

The smile that crossed the face of Dwan José Valdez was soon copied by his two outriders.

For some strange reason these men wanted Iron Eyes and the woman as their house guests.

As the bounty-hunter followed the trio of brightly decorated riders, he in turn being followed by the oxen pulling the wagon, he began to get worried.

They were heading inland. Away from the Rio Grande. Away from Texas. It was not where they wanted to go but for the time being they had little choice but to follow. For some reason, Iron Eyes felt that this might be his first big mistake, but knew killing these men might bring more *vaqueros* down on them instantly.

The sun was high overhead and burning down on all five members of the strange procession.

71

Iron Eyes had been correct. As they made their way, more and more *vaqueros* appeared from various points along their route. Soon more than twenty men wearing large sombreros completely surrounded them.

ELEVEN

The beautiful *hacienda* was vast, with a wide, over-hanging roof of red tiles. It stood away from the surrounding prairie yet seemed to match the area. It had that Latin look which made it appear to have always been there amongst the trees and cactus.

As the wagon rolled through the archway into the elegant courtyard a distant rumble of thunder seemed to echo a warning to the dark rider Iron Eyes. He kept looking at Jane as she effortlessly guided her team of proud oxen toward the walled stables.

The expression on the cigar-smoking Jane suddenly altered as her eyes saw the beautiful surroundings and absorbed every single feature of this place. It was a typical Mexican set-up. It was as if they had stumbled into a complete township in miniature, and Jane's eyes bulged trying to take everything in. She had never before seen flowers like the ones that grew on climbing vines around the courtyard.

The smell of cultured roses filled the air, and almost blocked out the aroma of horses and cattle.

This was indeed an oasis in an otherwise desolate place. They had been led ten miles from the rolling river to this place, and both Iron Eyes and his female companion were anxious. Neither were used to meeting people with good intentions and felt they had entered a possible trap.

The weathered bounty-hunter was quick to toss his long right leg over the saddle-horn before sliding down the saddle on to the dusty ground. His eyes were narrow and flashed around the many riders who surrounded him.

These were *vaqueros*. He had never before met any of them, and felt uneasy at their ability to talk without his ability to understand.

It was as if they all were dressed for church to the man who had seldom bothered to wash himself or his clothing. These men were, on the whole, immaculate. That worried him.

There were women around the *hacienda* courtyard, although they stayed mainly in the shadows, as if they required permission to step into the sun.

As Iron Eyes paced toward the wagon he could not believe the sight of so many silver objects attached to so many saddles. It was like looking into a treasure chest. Why on earth would these folks waste silver simply to decorate saddles? They were a rum bunch and he did not like rum bunches.

Jane sat on her wooden plank, still gripping the Winchester rifle on her lap. Still keeping her finger upon the trigger as she too studied the scene.

Then they heard the music.

Both Jane and Iron Eyes were shocked that guitars could be played outside a music hall. Yet they were. The small group of men were strumming their various sized guitars and singing up on an elevated porch.

'What the hell have we ridden into, Iron Eyes?' Jane spat at the ground as she watched the men dismounting.

'Beats me,' he shrugged.

'I heard of circuses but never thought I'd see one.' She gave a subtle laugh at their hosts' expense.

Iron Eyes continued to look about the courtyard and still could not feel easy with their situation.

'What you reckon is going on?'

'I figure we are in trouble, big trouble.' She sniffed at the men who made her feel rather less than feminine.

Iron Eyes reached up a long, thin arm and took her hand as she climbed slowly down with her trusty rifle in her hand. As she reached the ground she resumed her grip upon the weapon.

Dwan José Valdez dismounted and made his way toward the pair of curious Americans.

'You are still not trusting me?' he asked, taking off his wide sombrero and giving it to a servant.

'This don't make no sense, Valdez.' Jane chewed on her words as he came to a stop before them. Her eyes took him in. From his polished boots to his oiled hair. 'This is some kinda trick.'

Valdez gave a sigh. 'This is no trick, dear lady.'

'What do you want to invite us here for?' Iron Eyes' voice was low, and almost inaudible.

'You were on my land. You are my guests,' the Mexican smiled.

'It don't figure,' she told the man.

Valdez gave a respectful look at her rifle. 'My men used to shoot anyone who strayed on to my *rancho*, but I tell them it is not civilized.'

'True.' Iron Eyes watched as the majority of the *vaqueros* disappeared into various buildings around the courtyard. Soon there were only a handful left. All elegant. All standing behind Valdez.

The fingers of Dwan José clicked, and from nowhere a female servant appeared at his side. The man spoke to the girl, and then turned to Jane and translated.

'I tell her to take you to my best guest room where you can bathe and refresh yourself before our evening meal.'

Jane glanced at Iron Eyes, who was still watching the *vaqueros* over the Mexican's shoulder. He cast his eyes down upon her for an instant, before returning his attention to the men before him.

'What you reckon, Iron Eyes?' You could cut Jane's suspicions with a knife.

'Go get yourself pampered,' he advised, as he saw an entire steer being prepared for placing upon a giant roasting spit near a large wall.

Without hesitation she followed the servant along to the tiled steps that led to the elevation and arched porch. With every step Jane took she looked at a different face, as if searching for the one who was going to kill her.

'Your woman will feel wonderful after Bonita fixes her a bath,' Valdez said with a cheery smile.

'She ain't my woman,' Iron Eyes said, almost regretfully.

'No?' The older man tilted his head. 'I think that you are mistaken, my tall *amigo*.'

'What ya mean?' Iron Eyes concentrated upon the man before him.

'I see the way she looks at you and the way you look at her.'

'So?'

'I forget you are not Mexican,' Valdez shrugged. 'We see things that you *gringos* seem to miss.'

Iron Eyes bit his lip. 'How long are we your guests?'

'Why are you so concerned, my tall friend?'

'It comes natural.'

Iron Eyes allowed himself to be led in the same direction that Jane had taken a few minutes earlier. He knew that every eye was upon him, and wondered how many rifle sights had him dead to rights as he ascended the tiled steps.

He found himself in a large, cool, roof-top room with a massive bed and a simple crucifix upon a bare white wall. The shorter Mexican clapped his hands, and two servants brought in a large tin bath whilst others followed with jugs of steaming water and towels.

Iron Eyes stood speechless as he watched the men quickly preparing his bath. The trouble was, he did not like baths or bathing or water for that matter.

The perfume that they added seemed to lather up as they continued to arrive with more and yet more jugs of steaming hot water.

Valdez pointed to the bed, where a black suit of clothes were laid complete with frilly white shirt and red scarf.

'For you to wear whilst your clothes are washed and dried by my servants,' Valdez beamed.

Iron Eyes gritted his teeth.

'I don't like baths.'

'But think about the lady.' Valdez gestured with his arms.

'What?' Iron Eyes was confused.

'She bathes for you.'

'So?' Iron Eyes tried to seem uninterested in

what Jane was doing, but failed to convince his host.

'Then would not a gentleman do likewise?'

Iron Eyes rubbed his neck and became suddenly aware of the filth on it. 'I ain't exactly what you could call a gentleman, Valdez.'

'But you must not disappoint her.'

'Guess not,' Iron Eyes found himself muttering.

The tall man, who was thinner than most of his deceased victims, started to disrobe slowly. Very slowly. The servants vanished, leaving only the bounty-hunter and his host in the room. The long coat was dropped to the floor, sending a cloud of trail-dust rising. Then he took his Navy Colts out of his belt and placed them beside the clothes.

Dwan José grinned at the pain his guest was suffering just removing the garments which were almost like a second skin to him.

'That water better not be hot,' Iron Eyes growled. 'I ain't partial to hot water.'

'After you bathe, it will be you who will be hot,' Valdez said as he left the veranda door. 'Hot for the lady.'

Iron Eyes felt very uneasy. Yet the Latin might just be right about the effect a good wash might have on Jane. Cautiously, he dipped his toe into the tub. It was a sensation that was truly alien to the tall man. But hell, he had started, so he figured he might as well continue.

TWELVE

The Rio Grande was no longer swollen as the two riders reached its bank. Tom Hardy dropped from his horse and held on to the reins as he tried to make out the tracks. The sun had set thirty minutes earlier, and it was getting darker with every passing second.

'We better camp here for the night, Whit,' the elder Hardy brother shouted at his sibling, over the noise of the river as it continued its never-ending flow.

Whit crawled down from his saddle and flopped on to the sandy ground.

'Get some kindling for a fire,' Tom ranted, as he tied up his horse to a tree-branch.

'What for?' Whit drawled.

'For a fire so we don't freeze to death,' Tom said, as he then tied up his brother's horse. He started to untie the horse's belly-straps before dragging off the saddle.

'I hurt.' Whit rubbed his inner thighs with his rough hands.

'So do I,' Tom shouted, as he started upon the second saddle with tired hands.

'Not as bad as me.'

Tom Hardy took great delight in kicking his brother until the man got back on to his feet and started to gather firewood from the sand around them.

Soon they had enough, and the fire was set. Soon they had a roaring blaze to sit before, with their stinking horse blankets wrapped around their shoulders.

The two men watched the bacon frying in their pan. The smell was good.

A coffee-pot was hung over the flames that surrounded the cast-iron pan.

Neither man had eaten all day. Now they were tired from riding and drinking. The stars above their heads were brighter than usual, and they could feel the frost gripping the edge of their blankets as they waited for their food to cook.

'Reckon that varmint crossed here, Tom?' drawled Whit, as his mouth drooled.

'Couldn't make out his tracks.' Tom rattled the pan and added more wood. 'Too damn dark when we got here. But I got a feeling in my guts that he wouldn't have managed to cross that river.'

'Why not?'

'Well, if he had tried to cross that I figure he

done got himself drowned.' Tom hoped that was the case.

'I ain't gonna cross this river here, Tom,' Whit shrugged as the sound of the rolling waves filled his ears.

'Why not, boy?'

'You know I can't swim.' Whit rubbed his nose upon his sleeve.

'All you gotta do is hang on to the saddle-horn, Whit.'

'What if the horse drowns?'

'Good point,' Tom Hardy grinned. 'That tequila must be doing your brain good.'

'Reckon?'

'Yep. You are usually a lot dumber than this.'

Whit Hardy swigged at his bottle and accepted a large slice of red-hot bacon on his tin plate. Both men ate and drank their fill.

Tom Hardy drank coffee whilst his young brother finished off his third bottle. Now Tom knew he would have to hand over his three tequila bottles to the youth. It always worked that way.

As the snoring filled his ears, Tom Hardy lay on the soft ground thinking about Iron Eyes. The thoughts kept him awake for a long time.

THIRTEEN

The *hacienda* was illuminated by a vast array of bright lanterns that seemed to fill every possible corner and cranny. The music was now even more emotive, and filled the perfumed air of the courtyard.

Dancing seemed to be what these Mexicans enjoyed best, and it was all totally different to anything that the pair of *gringos* had ever experienced before.

The meal had been little less than a feast, and the wine had flowed like water. It was as if there was an endless supply of everything on this ranch.

The roasted steer was still being turned by the small group of cooks over the fire. A quarter had already been eaten by the people of the *hacienda*. It had even tempted the bounty-hunter with its aroma and taste.

The laughter and joy that this place seemed to

represent was strange compared to the simple, hard lives both Iron Eyes and Jane had previously experienced.

She had been washed and dressed by the female servants in a beautiful dress of thin, frilly layers. She had had her long hair washed and dressed until she looked almost to have Mexican blood herself. Even the red flower behind her ear seemed to be totally suitable for her.

All Jane lacked was the smile that seemed to ooze from every other female face on the *rancho*.

Jane looked the part though. She looked like a woman for the first time in a very long time. Although she would never admit it to either herself or anyone else, it made her feel good. Yet even as she walked in her flowing, light dress across the cool, tiled floor in her bare feet, she felt uneasy and still wondered why they had been brought here.

What could their motives be, to grab a pair of dusty strangers off a riverbank and bring them to your home? To treat them as if they were honoured guests? Charity was something neither she nor the tall, grim bounty-hunter knew anything about, so this was the one factor that eluded their suspicious minds.

The sight of Iron Eyes with his black suit and white shirt made her gasp when she first saw him entering the dining-room. Now, as they walked along in the moonlight in the sheltered courtyard of the beautiful *hacienda*, she was almost used to the strange sight.

His hair was clean and combed back off his face, showing the scars that smallpox had made during his tormented childhood. Yet he was clean and that seemed odd. Not only to Jane but to himself.

The smell of stale sweat tends to become part of one's persona when it remains long enough, now the smell had been replaced by the aroma of perfumed water. Iron Eyes was understandably very nervous. His nostrils did not recognize his own body.

It was as if he were naked. He had washed away his identity. Now he tried to remain above what was happening in this place. It had to be some sort of trap. Nobody could convince the tall, gaunt man to alter his mind. The only thing that he was grateful to Valdez about was the beef meal. It lay on his stomach better than all the chilli and hard tack he had consumed over the past weeks of trailing Dan Hardy.

She had left her Winchester in the room whilst Iron Eyes had stuffed his Navy Colts into his belt sash. He trusted nobody in this strange place, and felt like shooting someone to see what might happen.

How he had managed to resist shooting anyone was a mystery to himself. The water of the bath must have softened his brains as well as his skin, he assumed.

Iron Eyes leaned on the white-washed wall that looked over the landscaped gardens and court-yard. He knew that this was a trap in his guts. Even filled with well-cooked beef and delicious wine, his natural instincts would not allow him to drop his guard for even a second.

Jane seemed to be enjoying being pampered, but the bounty-hunter knew that you got nothing for nothing in this life. At least, he had never experienced anything to make him alter his mind.

The scene was tranquil and peaceful, but this did not sit easily in Iron Eyes' mind. His hands were never far from his guns as he tried to appear relaxed.

In truth he was ready to draw and start shoot-ing if anything provoked him. Anything at all.

Pausing to witness the festivities, the two stud-ied each other in the light of the countless lanterns.

'You ain't bad-looking,' Jane said.

'Thanks,' Iron Eyes nodded.

Jane waited for a long time for him to return the compliment, but that was something that did not enter his head.

'Do I look OK?' she hinted.

His grey eyes briefly glanced at her before returning to the scene around and below them.

'You smell good.'

She decided that was as good as it would get. Compliments were not his strength. He kept touching the handles of his guns with his thumbs as the music filled their ears.

'They seem so happy, Iron Eyes,' Jane sighed. 'I guess I am feeling a lot better than I did when I shot that hole out of your ear.'

Iron Eyes touched the scab thoughtfully. 'If you had been a man you'd be dead now, Jane.'

She gave him a smile that seemed almost feminine. 'This seems a real happy place.'

'Ain't natural,' he snapped.

'Not at all natural,' she agreed.

'You trust this Dwan José Valdez varmint?' he eventually asked.

'Guess so,' Jane answered, after giving the situation a lot of thought. She had never been treated like this. She felt almost regal with her full stomach.

'Wish I could.' Iron Eyes shook his head slowly as he absorbed anything and everything. 'But I just can't.'

FOURTEEN

Dawn crept across the now calm Rio Grande river, sending the sunlight flashing around the two brothers who were huddled together. No longer raging in fury, the water was now little more than three feet deep. The bright rays woke Tom Hardy first, and he scrambled to his feet to stretch the cramp out of his aching joints. It had been cold during his sleep, and he felt older than his years as he paced around, trying to get his legs to loosen up before waking his drunken brother.

Then he saw them across the water.

It had been the glinting of sunlight upon their lances that first caught his eye. He tried to make out what he had not previously noticed – the band of Apache sitting astride their painted ponies – and his brain desperately attempted to figure out what he should do next.

His mouth was dry from the crippling sleep, but now it was getting worse as fear raced through his body. He kneeled down next to the snoring

Whit and shook his brother feverishly. It was never easy waking Whit at the best of times, but somehow the urgency in Tom Hardy's hands penetrated Whit's blurred mind, managing to get him out of his drunken dreams. The whites of the younger Hardy's eyes were raked with red veins as he gazed up in befuddled apathy.

'Apache,' Tom whispered. His voice was shaking so much that he had barely been able to say that one simple word.

His younger brother got on to his elbows and gave Tom a confused stare.

'What about them?' Whit asked, rubbing the sleep and sand from the corners of his sore eyes.

Tom indicated with his head at the group of men across the river.

Whit focused on the Indians and then looked up into Tom's face for answers.

'What we gonna do?' he asked in a lowered tone, as if the braves might be able to overhear their conversation across the breaking waves of the wide river.

'I don't know,' Tom croaked.

'I wish Dan was here,' Whit said, as he slowly turned over on his side and searched for his gun.

'So do I.' Tom kept his back to the river and the band of curious braves. 'He was a better shot than either of us.'

'Reckon they are friendly?' Whit checked his pistol to see if he had remembered to load it. To his surprise, he had. Although he had no memory of when and where he had done so.

Tom Hardy rose to his feet, still clutching on to his blanket as he moved toward their horses. He studied the Indians more closely from the cover of the bushes and tree.

There were only five men, dressed in a combination of styles that ranged from Mexican farmer to native tribesman. Their hats gave their identities away though. Only Apache wore feathers in their ten-gallon hats. Only Apache had long black hair that always seemed to have been sheered in a straight line at shoulder-length. The lances too bore eagle feathers tied with dyed grass from just below the sharpened steel points.

Unlike the tribes to the north, who frequented the vast, endless plains, the Apache never seemed very intimidating by the way they dressed, but these were probably the most dangerous of Indians that any white men could encounter. They were not easily fooled by trinkets, and would fight to the death. These were the men who sat watching the two Hardy brothers from their small ponies.

Tom indicated to his brother to join him behind the cover of the tree, which Whit duly did.

'I can't see any rifles,' Tom said, pointing at the quintet of Apache braves.

'That don't mean they ain't got any.' Whit sniffed as he too watched the silent observers.

Tom raised his eyebrows as he rested his arms on the back of his brother's horse. His belly was grumbling for breakfast and coffee but this was not the time or place to consider getting domestic.

'But it might.' Tom rubbed his rough hairy chin as he tried to get his brain around their problem.

'Apache without rifles?' Whit shook his head. 'I think you're crazy. Dang crazy.'

'Start to saddle up,' Tom said, as he grabbed his younger sibling by the ear. 'Try not to let them see you doing it.'

'What you going to do, Tom?' Whit enquired, as the older man stepped toward the two saddles upon the ground by the bushes.

Tom slid his Winchester out of its sheath and pulled out a box of cartridges from his saddle-bag. He started forcing the shells into the rifle, cranking its lever with every insertion.

'I'm going to sit by this tree and give us some cover whilst you get them saddles on to them horses, boy,' Tom replied. 'So get them saddles on to them horses fast.'

'How come you get to cover me and I gotta do all the work?'

'Maybe because I can shoot straighter than you, Whit.'

'Only a tad straighter,' Whit grumbled as he folded the blankets and tossed them over the backs of their horses.

Tom Hardy knelt down by the tree and leaned

into its trunk as he held the fully loaded repeating rifle in his sweating hands.

The Apache looked like statues as they sat upon their ponies watching the two men. Only their long black hair moved as the breeze off the fast-flowing river blew it around their shoulders.

FIFTEEN

Twenty miles away in the warmth of the room within Dwan José Valdez's *hacienda*, Iron Eyes awoke in terror. He lay for an instant upon his back on the soft, clean bed, staring at the white ceiling above his head. His steel-grey pupils studied the cracks in the plaster as his mind raced. His head felt foggy as he lay upon the bed, then he recalled the wine. The ever-flowing wine of the previous evening.

Then his highly tuned senses became aware of the reason he had woken so suddenly from a deep slumber.

The aroma of a cigar had drifted across him, filling his nostrils.

Iron Eyes knew that he was not alone.

Turning his head slightly, he focused upon the seated figure of Valdez. He had two *vaqueros* standing behind him, holding their .45s across their hearts. They were emotionless as they stood guard over their master. Only their blinking black eyes moved as they watched the prostrate man.

They were ready for action even if he was not.

Iron Eyes moved his hands toward the handles of his Navy Colts, but they were no longer tucked into the sash around his slim waist. Sitting upright in one quick movement, his eyes searched around the bed for the missing guns.

For the first time in a long while, panic raced through Iron Eyes. Without his guns he was just another tall, thin human being with a pitted face.

Valdez raised his hands from his lap and waved the two Navy Colts in the air.

'Looking for these, my very tall friend?' the elegant man asked as his white teeth gripped the long cigar.

'How did you get my irons, Valdez?' Iron Eyes growled. 'No living creature can touch my guns without me knowing.'

'You did drink the wine that was left by your bed, did you not?' Dwan José pointed at the empty bottle on a stand next to the bed. The bottle was almost empty.

'Sure, but I wasn't drunk enough for you to get my guns off me.' Iron Eyes swung his long legs over the edge of the bed and planted his bare feet upon the cold, tiled floor. Apart from his socks and boots, the bounty-hunter was still fully dressed.

'That was no normal bottle of wine, Mister Iron

Eyes.' The smart man smiled at the confused bounty-hunter.

'It was drugged?' Iron Eyes ran his hands through his long hair as he stared at the trio before him. 'You drugged my booze and I was dumb enough to drink it. Great.'

'Just a little sleeping potion, my tall friend,' Dwan José shrugged.

'I knew it.' Iron Eyes shook his head angrily. 'I knew that it was some sort of trick. I ain't no outlaw so you've caught yourself someone with no price on his head, Valdez.'

'What?' Valdez seemed offended. 'What do you mean?'

'The kindness. I knew it was a trick.' Iron Eyes cupped his head in his wide, bony hands as he tried to console himself at being captured, not the hunter, for once in his life.

'My generosity is not a trick.' Valdez stood in fury. 'I did not trick you. I am the most generous man in all Mexico.'

'Then how come you got my shooting irons?' Iron Eyes also stood up, but was too wise to make a move on the three men who had not only their own guns but his too.

Valdez seemed suddenly sad as he tossed the Navy Colts on to the bed beside the tall man. Iron Eyes looked at his guns which were now within his reach with a confused expression upon his face.

'You steal my guns then give them back?' Iron Eyes narrowed his eyes as he stood watching the man. 'I don't get it.'

'Do not worry, my friend. They are not loaded. I am not a fool,' Valdez said as he puffed on his cigar. 'I have a favour to ask of you.'

'Favour?' The word did not rest easy in Iron Eyes' guts. He had a code that required payment for everything he did.

'You are well known to my people.' Valdez seated himself back down and watched as the bounty-hunter followed suit. 'You are the famous hunter of men. You are the man who can kill without any fear or regret. We have no such person here.'

'I'm Iron Eyes, if that's what you mean.'

'Exactly. You are Iron Eyes.' Valdez flicked ash on to the floor, and then stared hard into the eyes of the stranger before him. 'I require your services. I shall pay you much gold coin for you to do a job for me.'

'You want someone killed?' Iron Eyes found himself grinning in expectation.

'Not exactly. Although I think that your skill in that area might be called upon.' Valdez ran his fingers nervously over the long moustache as if trying to find the words he required.

'I ain't no gunslinger. I ain't no hired gun,' Iron Eyes informed the man. 'I hunt bounty on varmints. Dead or alive.'

Valdez leaned forward. 'You are a man who can face other men and overcome all odds, my tall friend. You are a man like no other. This is what I require.'

'I'm good at what I do.'

'I knew you were heading for the Rio Grande before you left Texas,' Valdez said bluntly. 'I have my spies. I have something for you to consider.'

'Spit it out.' Iron Eyes rubbed his chin as he concentrated on the neat Mexican.

'My daughter was taken by bandits over ten days ago.' The man was unashamed of the tears which swelled up in his mature eyes and started to roll down his face as he spoke.

'Taken?' Iron Eyes sat upright. 'You mean that bandits kidnapped your daughter?'

'Yes, my tall friend.' Valdez pulled in on his cigar and then blew the grey smoke at the floor. 'My only daughter Maria was taken from my personal coach. My *vaqueros* were outnumbered, and all but two lost their lives trying to protect her. My men are as brave as lions but they are not killers.'

'How many *vaqueros* were guarding your daughter?' Iron Eyes was becoming more and more curious.

'Ten.' Valdez shook his head at the floor, sending a shower of tears descending to his feet.

'The bandits killed eight of your men just to get your daughter?' Iron Eyes spoke in a tone that spelled his disgust for the bandits.

'Yes.'

Iron Eyes rubbed his neck. 'You know who these men are?'

The older man nodded. 'I have received a ransom letter with a lock of Maria's hair. They want gold.'

'Why not pay them instead of hiring me?' Iron Eyes asked.

'Because they will simply do it again and again.' Valdez seemed to know something about these bandits that he had not yet conveyed to the bounty-hunter. 'You will stop them ever doing it again.'

'Then I'll get your daughter from them.' Iron Eyes stood as if suddenly charged with energy. He picked up his saddle-bags and emptied their contents upon the bed. The boxes of bullets were quickly swooped up by his long fingers. He started to insert them one by one into his Navy Colts.

'How much money do you want, my tall one?'

'Half of whatever those varmints demanded in the ransom note,' Iron Eyes grunted.

'Only half?' Valdez stood and offered the man a cigar, which was accepted.

'Half will be fine.' Iron Eyes bit off the end of his cigar and rammed it into his mouth as he accepted a light from the smaller man.

Dwan José stood and bowed his head. 'I am sorry about drugging your wine, my tall friend,

98

but I had to ensure that you would still be here this morning. I required time for us to talk.'

'That wine tasted pretty good.' Iron Eyes almost smiled as he took in a lungful of the strong smoke.

SIXTEEN

The saddles were on and Whit Hardy leaned over his horse at his brother, who sat watching the Apache who watched them.

'Ready, Tom,' he reluctantly said. He might have a hangover straight from hell itself but he was sober enough to be very worried at what might happen in the next few minutes of their futile lives. He knew that his sibling was correct – he could not hit the side of a barn with his gun, and had only ever been useful to Dan at firing in the air outside banks they were robbing, in an action known as 'clearing the streets'. If Whit had to shoot at Indians charging at them, it was likely that Tom was going to get hit before the warriors.

Tom Hardy slowly rose to his feet, keeping the rifle close to his chest, as he moved backward toward the saddled mounts.

Whit mounted, staying behind the bushes to conceal his actions as his elder brother cautiously took hold of the reins in his free hand. It was just as he lifted his leg and slid his pointed boot into the stirrup that the Indians suddenly became animated and very, very loud.

The small band of Apache were charging through the river toward them, screaming at the top of their high-pitched voices. It was a sound that could freeze the blood of any normal man, and both the Hardy brothers were very normal.

Somehow, Tom managed to get his leg over the horse and get into the saddle.

He pulled the horse's neck around as far as it would go and started, before aiming at the long trail that edged the river down toward Mexico. Sinking their spurs into their horses' flesh, they rode away from their camp.

The two riders thundered along the sandy embankment as the Apache finally got across the wide river, and began giving chase to them.

A shot passed over Tom Hardy's Stetson as he kept pace with his younger brother in their desperate gallop along the trail.

'They got rifles, Tom!' Whit yelled, as another shot whistled past them. 'I told you they had rifles!'

'Guess so,' Tom Hardy agreed as he tried to give his horse its head as well as slide his Winchester back into its sheath.

The warriors were chasing the pair at top speed along the rough terrain and letting rip with their rifles. For them to ride and shoot was something

101

they learned as children, whereas the Hardy brothers had difficulty in doing one thing at a time, let alone two.

For them, to ride and stay in the saddle was an achievement to brag about. They had been chased by the odd posse before, but never by Indians.

Forging their way through a wall of tall bushes that strayed in front of them, the two brothers managed to stay in their saddles. More shots filled the air, and were closer than either man liked.

It seemed that they would have to ride to the far-off ocean before these Indians would quit. Blood filled the air as they continued to spur their galloping mounts into finding speed that neither animal knew it possessed.

The chase went on for over two miles along the river's edge, before the young Apache braves pulled their ponies to a halt and then started laughing at the fleeing pair of white men. They had had their fun, and returned to the campsite to see what the men had discarded in their hasty departure.

For Whit and Tom Hardy it would be another few miles before they figured that their pursuers were no longer behind them. Then another mile or so before they felt confident enough to slow up and eventually stop.

Then another hour or so before they realized that they were looking at the tracks of Iron Eyes' unshod pony, plus a wagon.

The two men drank their fill of the river before setting off after the man who had killed their brother Dan. The wagon tracks were a confusion to the two men, but neither bothered themselves about it.

They were just thankful that they had saved their scalps and one full bottle of tequila.

SEVENTEEN

Dwan José Valdez looked at his prized watch, which bore a small photograph of his beloved daughter Maria inside its golden case-lid. It was almost eight, and the morning sunshine was beginning to find its way into the *hacienda* court-yard.

Iron Eyes had exchanged his small pony for one of the *rancho* thoroughbreds. It was a large, black animal with a strong back and even stronger legs. The bounty-hunter stood in his freshly washed and dried clothes. The long coat had defied all attempts to clean off the years of dried blood-stains.

The master of the *hacienda* watched as the man with the limp, shoulder-length hair filled his deep pockets with cartridges for his Navy Colts and his Winchester.

Iron Eyes tucked his pistols into his belt with the handles facing outward.

Valdez moved toward the man who had been

given the job of hunting down the bandits who
had kidnapped his daughter.

'You are a very brave man, my tall friend,'
Valdez said in a humble voice.

'I ain't brave, Dwan José,' Iron Eyes said. 'I'm
edgy.'

'What is this edgy?' The mature man looked
surprised.

'I ain't killed anyone in a few days.' Iron Eyes
tried to force a grin but failed. 'I get edgy when I
ain't killed anyone for a few days.'

Valdez watched as the tall, painfully thin man
stepped into his stirrup and hoisted himself on to
the large, black stallion.

'You have my prayers travelling with you.'

'Hell, don't tell God what I'm up to, he might
not like it.' Iron Eyes gathered up the long,
beaded reins, turned the animal toward the archway of the *hacienda*, and for a moment paused.

'What is wrong?' Valdez asked with concern in
his voice as he walked to the rider.

Iron Eyes gave the beautiful building a long
look before gazing down at the elderly man. He
said nothing as he tapped his spurs into the horse
and rode out of the courtyard.

Dwan José watched with a few of his trusted
vaqueros at his side as the strange man disappeared down the long trail. He was headed south,
to the far-off mountains that were the boundary of
his vast ranch. The mountains where the bandits

105

hid from the federal soldiers. The mountains where until now, they had been safe.

Iron Eyes felt strange to be astride such a proud beast, and rode with more consideration than he normally gave his usual horses.

The mountains were getting ever closer as he increased the pace of the animal. This was no ordinary horse between his thin legs. He could feel the strength and power as the black creature thundered through the prairie desolation.

Iron Eyes knew that this was not like any job he had ever undertaken before. This job required him to try and bring back a person alive.

Normally he would just go in with his guns blazing, and to hell with any fool that didn't have the sense to duck. Maria Valdez might already be lying somewhere, being ripped apart by the buzzards, but if she was still alive he had to try and make sure she stayed that way.

He had seen the wanted posters that told him little about his prey except that they were scum.

Iron Eyes knew that the leader was a strange creature, with a distinctive gold tooth that dominated his face. He was nicknamed 'The Snake'.

The image from the wanted poster was imprinted upon the mind of the ruthless bounty-hunter as he steered the impressive horse through the chaparral toward the mountain range.

He had been riding for several hours and had noted the sun was now at its highest point. The trail that the Valdez family had carved out from the desert floor was just slightly wider than the average stagecoach. This, he had been advised by the elegant Dwan José, was the route that his coach was on that fateful day. Iron Eyes rode at an incredible pace upon the fine stallion that was so black that the cactus that verged the trail were almost reflected in its coat. Then he started to slow up as he saw what he had been searching for.

The coach was upon its side. It was twisted out of shape, and there were signs that a fire had been started beneath it. The black scorch-marks ended about a third of the way along the side of the once expensively decorated vehicle.

Iron Eyes had trouble controlling his mount as they approached the scene. The acrid stench of rotting horse-flesh filled the air with millions of huge flies.

Even the hard-gutted bounty-hunter found the smell more than he could take, and turned his head away in an attempt to get some clean air into his lungs. It was a smell that would not go away, and Iron Eyes tried three times to turn his horse toward the coach and its decomposing team before he managed to get the huge creature to trot past the scene.

The thin man, who resembled a skeleton himself, kept digging his spurs into the sides of the black horse until they had passed the destroyed coach.

With every stride his mount took, Iron Eyes studied the ground with an intensity equalled only by an eagle on the wing seeking out prey.

Then he saw the remnants of tracks in the deep, sandy soil. To anyone with ordinary vision, the few remaining marks would have been dismissed as just weathering. To Iron Eyes though, these marks told a familiar story.

As quickly as a flash he had dismounted and was on his knees, touching the soil with the long bony fingers of his left hand, as he gripped his reins tightly with his right.

The stallion was still spooked by the smell of the slaughtered beasts around the wrecked coach as well as the swarming flies that made a deafening noise above them.

Iron Eyes was silent as he stood and gazed through the broken undergrowth. He knew that this was the way that the bandits had left the scene with their prized captive.

He had followed men across much less hospitable terrain than this in order to claim the bounty upon their heads. Iron Eyes grabbed on to the saddle-horn and swung himself back up on to the high horse.

For another hour as he headed relentlessly through the dark blue sage and tumbleweed of the desert floor in the direction of the far-off mountain range, Iron Eyes sensed his quarry was close at hand. The soft sand drifted under the stallion's hooves as the heavy creature continued on.

The burning sun was now getting lower in the midday sky, and the rider was casting a giant shadow that stretched for hundreds of yards as he encouraged his horse forward, toward the golden range of mountains ahead.

Then suddenly his keen vision spotted something ahead, catching the bright sunlight. Iron Eyes stood in his stirrups until the stallion finally trotted to a stop. Dismounting, the tall, lean man led the horse toward the glinting object that was protruding from the sand.

It was amazing that he had spotted it, but his was no ordinary eyesight. Studying the ground he knew that many horses had recently passed along this trail.

Stooping down, his thin hand plucked up the tiny silver trinket, and looked at it hard and long.

Iron Eyes considered the object for several moments. It was a simple locket that had become separated from its chain. His long nails prized it open and then he knew that he was on the right trail. Two tiny trimmed photographs looked up at his narrow grey eyes. One was of a beautiful lady and the other of a young man. It was obvious that the image of the young man was Dwan José Valdez in his youth.

Iron Eyes gripped the tiny silver locket in his fist and smiled to himself. He knew that this was definitely the route that the bandits had taken when they had captured the young Maria. She had either lost this prized jewel accidentally, or had deliberately dropped it in a vain hope that it would help someone trying to help her escape from her captors.

Slipping the locket quickly into one of his deep pockets along with his bullets before mounting the stallion, he once more felt the blood raging into his fingers. He knew that he would soon get a chance to use his guns. This time he would also be trying to rescue a female, and that was something totally out of character. Now he was certain where to go.

He sat in his saddle, staring at the far-away mountains and their golden colour. He had heard that this land was filled with gold just waiting to be picked up off the ground. Iron Eyes adjusted the reins in his hands before starting off once more.

The mountains climbed up from the flat desert ahead of him as he spurred his mount onward.

With every hoof beat he felt his prey getting closer.

As he allowed the stallion to find his own pace, the bounty-hunter drew out one of his pistols and held it in his hand.

Soon he would be entering the mountains.

There it would take every ounce of his skill and accuracy with his weapons.

110

As he had informed Dwan José Valdez earlier, he had not killed anyone for a few days. Now every sinew of his being could sense the excitement that the chase and the eventual kill brought.

Nothing could replace the basic instinct of a hunter and, above all else, he was a hunter. A hunter of men.

Iron Eyes had death riding on his shoulder once more.

Death had been with him for many years.

He was used to his company.

EIGHTEEN

The golden mountain range was vast, like the country itself. Box canyons and endless trails that were natural mazes made this place safe for the bandit gang that had occupied it for the past few years after being driven north by the federal army of Cortez. Here they had built a handful of wooden shacks and created a small haven for themselves amid the arid mountainous boulders that made up the rocky range.

The Snake, as he was known, was their leader. He had killed all his opposition, and the remaining dozen or so bandits that remained were loyal to him until someone stronger and even more unscrupulous came along.

He was a well-built man who prided himself on his strength and sexual prowess. The Snake had been given his name by his fellow bandits for his ability to capture and bite the heads of any variety of snake they offered him.

He had been bitten by many snakes and had

112

never succumbed to their deadly poison. It was as if he were immune. This was why he ruled his mainly superstitious followers so easily.

To them the Snake was no mere man. He was touched by magic.

A magic that protected him.

They had raided as far away as Texas for what they required, and they required a lot. Money was always useful but gold or silver was their first true love. With gold and silver you could cross the border and obtain things that were unavailable in Mexico. When they wanted food they would seldom buy it, as they knew all the right places to steal anything and everything they needed.

They had brought many women to this secret place since they had established it. Women to cook for them. Women to wash their dirty clothes and keep the shacks clean. Women to lie down and lift their long skirts whenever they wanted to prove themselves.

Any women who found themselves pregnant were disposed of and quickly replaced. The Snake did not like children, even if his actions had created them. The foot-hills were littered with the skeletons of females whose services were no longer required by the bandit's leader.

The Snake had bedded all the women in his camp, and treated them for what they were. To him they were nothing he could not replace with a younger and better one. Some of these women had chosen to enter the bandit camp willingly, others had been taken from their loved ones and were mere slaves.

To the Snake, it was horses that were of true value, and he regretted that his men had killed so many whilst capturing the young Maria. He always treated his horse-flesh far better than he treated the camp females.

A horse gave you the means of escape whilst a woman, however good in bed, was like a millstone around his neck. Steal a woman and nobody cared too much, but steal a horse and the sentence was hanging. Even the law agreed with the Snake, it seemed.

A woman was of little value here, but horses were important.

It had been over ten days since he had captured the young and beautiful Maria Valdez, and she had been treated in the same way as he treated the camp women. The only difference being that the Snake had kept this prize for himself and had not shared her with the other bandits.

Maria Valdez was not like any woman he or his followers had ever seen before. She was tall and slim, whereas the women around the camp were short and plump.

She was of noble blood and descended from the Spanish that had taken this land from the Indians. Her blood had not been mixed with the natives, as had so many. She still retained the looks of her forebears. This was why the Snake did not want to share her with his men. She was special, and very different from all the other women in camp.

She was his.

The Snake stood watching her from the doorway as she sobbed in the corner of his shack. She had cried for ten solid days.

He was getting used to it.

She still wore the dress that she had been wearing upon the coach when he attacked it. It had been elegant then, with its crushed red velvet and white lace trimmings. Now it was soiled with all of life's filth. It was torn where his hands had been. It was now hanging limply from her frame after he had torn away the thick petticoats and pantalets and ravaged her once-virginal flesh.

Maria was considering her life as being close to its end as she shook, watching the man who stood in the doorway. Death was now all she looked forward to. Only death could wash away the dirt that he had forced into her.

The taste of dirt in her mouth would haunt her forever.

She had seen her hand-servant raped before her very eyes by the Snake and his men. The young girl had been dead long before the last bandit had used her. The girl's clothes had been torn away by the camp women as trophies as she was tied over a boulder and used.

Maria knew that this image would also remain with her forever as she watched the Snake drooling at her once more. He had drunk his bottle of wine and was ready once more.

There had been so many bottles of wine, she thought.

Sobbing had become her only escape. The salt of her tears filled her mouth as she cringed in the corner awaiting his next assault. Maria prayed that the salt in her tears might take away the taste from her palate. She knew it was coming again soon. He was like a rampant breeding bull with little else on his mind. Tossing the empty bottle into the dirt, the Snake started to untie the knotted rope around his solid waist.

His laughter became so loud that it drowned out her terrified pleas for mercy.

This was not a man, it was a creature.

He had no emotions, only desires.

As she opened her wet, burning eyes, she saw him moving toward her once more. The gleaming gold tooth loomed over her once again as she watched him reaching out for her.

Her sobs became screams once again.

Yet once more her screams went unanswered.

NINETEEN

Dwan José Valdez was sitting alone beside the large fountain that drew fresh spring-water from deep below the *hacienda* and allowed it to cascade into the ornate raised trough. He ran his hand through the cool, crystal-clear water as the tall, strangely attractive Jane walked toward him.

Looking up from his thoughts the mature man nodded at her as she approached.

'I must have overslept.' She said as if she had provided an excuse for her waking up so late in the day.

Valdez knew the truth. He had drugged her wine as he had done with Iron Eyes. He did not want her rising before the lean bounty-hunter, and possibly preventing the man from going after the bandits who had captured his darling Maria. He knew that it was a terrible thing to do to a fellow human being, but his moral ethics could never compete with his duty as a parent. Iron Eyes was Valdez's only hope.

117

'You drank much wine last night, my dear.' He grinned.

'I did?' Jane sat next to him and rubbed the tight muscles in her neck. 'I can't recall.'

'It was a party,' Valdez shrugged. 'You had travelled far and were entitled to enjoy yourself.'

She agreed. 'It was enjoyable.'

Valdez felt guilty, but decided not to enlighten her too soon about what was occurring. Iron Eyes had been gone for several hours now, and with every second that passed drew closer to his destination.

'Is Iron Eyes still asleep in his room?' she enquired innocently.

Valdez took hold of her hand and looked at the hard skin upon its palm. This was a woman who worked. Worked hard.

'Iron Eyes is not here,' he said softly. As he had finished his short sentence he could feel the reaction in her hand. Suddenly it was tense. He held on to it and smoothed it tenderly, until he could see she had relaxed from the shock that her strange companion had left the *hacienda*.

'Where has he gone, Dwan José?' She stared hard at him.

'To the mountains,' he reluctantly replied, trying not to look her straight in the eyes.

She looked puzzled. 'Why would he go there?'

'For me,' Valdez sighed. 'He went there for me.'

'But why?' Jane could not get the fog out of her

brain as she tried to concentrate.

'Iron Eyes is a very brave man who has agreed to do a very important job for me, my dear.' The elderly man stood and focused on the trickling water that spurted from the top of his fine fountain.

'You say he is brave?' Jane looked up at the man with eyes that begged answers.

'I am not man enough to do what has to be done,' Valdez said quietly. 'Iron Eyes is. He has the heart of a lion.'

'What sort of danger is he riding into?' She grabbed at his sleeve, causing him to turn and look at her. 'And why is he risking himself for you?'

'He is trying to save my daughter's life. She was kidnapped by bandits ten days ago.' Valdez found his voice drying up, and was forced to cup his hands under the flowing water and drink.

'Iron Eyes is going up against a gang of bandits?' She felt a pain in her stomach. It was a pain caused by sudden anxiety.

'Exactly. As I said, he is a very brave man.'

'You have so many men here, why ask him?' Jane stood next to the man, who was visibly shaking.

'I have many *vaqueros* here, Jane.' Valdez bowed his head before looking through his eyebrows at her. 'Iron Eyes is not a mere *vaquero*, he is a hunter of men.'

She looked puzzled once more.

Valdez continued. 'He is my daughter's only hope.'

Jane suddenly looked very, very angry. 'You used Iron Eyes to save your daughter? He's going up against a gang of bandits who will probably cut him down before he gets close to them.'

'Have faith, my dear,' Valdez pleaded softly.

'Faith? In what?' She was glowing red with fury as she clenched her fists and struck Valdez upon his shoulder.

'Faith in the man you love,' Dwan José replied.

'How dare you say that?'

'Look at yourself, my dear,' Valdez sighed. 'Iron Eyes is a hunter. He has captured your heart, has he not?'

The tall female strolled away from him in silence as he brooded with his thoughts. Guilt crept over him once more as he realized that he might have sent Iron Eyes to his death. Casting an eye at Jane, Dwan José Valdez watched as she ascended the tiled steps. Taking another drink of water, he crossed himself and said a silent prayer.

TWENTY

Whit Hardy sat looking at the *hacienda* with a mixture of envy and distaste. Why would anyone want such a large house? His brother Tom was standing at his horse's head, pouring the last of his precious canteen water into his Stetson for the tired horse to drink.

Tom had been silent for a long time now. Whatever thoughts were passing through his brain, he was keeping them private.

Whit slid off his saddle on to the soft ground and copied his brother's actions. The horse could have his fill of the water as long as he still had some tequila left in his last bottle, Whit thought.

Tom Hardy watched as his kid brother watered the nag and drank the blinding clear liquor at the same time. He knew that it was his tequila Whit gulped, but he no longer gave a damn.

Sober or drunk, the situation was the same to Tom. They had run out of supplies and water, and the only place they could get fresh provisions was the *hacienda* before them. The *hacienda* that the tracks of their prey Iron Eyes led right into.

It was not the way he had planned it. The Apache had screwed everything into the ground. They had confused the elder Hardy brother and made him make errors.

He was starting to doubt himself even more than usual.

'The tracks lead straight into that place,' Tom said, looking at the white-washed *hacienda*. Sweat ran down his face as he spoke, and he knew that he had to make a decision soon.

Very soon, or they would have no chance of surviving.

'You reckon he's in there, Tom?' Whit asked, in his usual slurred way.

'Could be,' Tom answered as his horse finished the water, allowing him to return the Stetson on to his head.

'It don't figure.' Whit shook his hat free of the last few drops of water.

'What?'

'Why did he turn back from the river?' Whit knew that it seemed very out of character for the bounty hunter to be heading to the place he had to collect his reward, then change direction and ride into the desert. Everything he had ever heard about the strange Iron Eyes said that he would not have done this, yet he had.

'I wish I knew.' Tom Hardy was as puzzled as his sibling.

'He was heading for El Paso to collect his reward money.' Whit watched his exhausted horse licking the ground for further droplets of water. 'Then he turns and heads here. Why?'

'Maybe he had no choice,' Tom pondered.

'What you mean?' Whit scratched his head. 'This is the famous Iron Eyes I'm talking about, Tom.'

'What about all these horse and wagon tracks?' Tom pointed at the churned-up soil. 'He might have been forced to go with these people.'

'You reckon they are soldiers?' Whit Hardy became skittish at the thought of an army.

'Could be. There is a hell of a lot of them.' Tom mounted again and watched as his younger brother followed suit.

'So what we gonna do?' Whit looked at the remains of his bottle, and replaced the cork before sliding the glass into his shirt. 'What we gonna do?'

'Ride in.' Tom rubbed his face.

'Ride into that place?' Whit stood in his stirrups and pointed at the white building, his face twisted in horror at the thought of entering. It felt too much like suicide.

'We gotta ride in, boy,' Tom snapped angrily. His temper was not aimed at his brother but at himself for getting them into this situation.

123

'Why?' Whit continued to look troubled.

'We gotta get water, ain't we?' Tom spurred his horse forward and looked over his shoulder at Whit following. 'We gotta get grub, ain't we? Come on.'

'This is crazy, Tom,' Whit protested.

'Not as crazy as dying of thirst,' Tom snarled again. 'I seen folks that died of thirst, and it ain't a nice sight.'

'But what if Iron Eyes is in there?' Whit knew that the bounty-hunter would recognize them from the wanted posters they shared with their late brother Dan. 'He'll kill us on sight.'

'We have to take our chances.'

'Why?'

'We might live long enough to kill him, Whit.' Tom rubbed his grumbling guts as he rode. 'Besides, I am so hungry that the thought of getting shot don't worry me at all.'

The two horsemen rode slowly. Very slowly indeed. This was a journey that neither of them wanted to make, but both knew that they had no option.

The sun was low, and there was a chill in the air. As they rode they could see men at the *hacienda* lighting torches at the arched gateway. Then they could hear the excited shouting within the courtyard.

They had been spotted.

Both men's hearts sank as they witnessed the

dozen or so *vaqueros* riding to meet them. The elegant riders in their wide sombreros were soon close enough that the Hardy brothers could see the sweat upon their darkly tanned faces.

Tom reined his mount to a halt first, sending a cloud of trail-dust into the still air. Whit pulled up his nag at his brother's side with the terrified expression of a sand fox cornered by a puma upon his face.

His eyes flashed from one *vaquero* to another as Valdez's men rode nearer and nearer.

'Easy, boy!' Tom yelled at his brother, who was fumbling for his .45. 'Leave your iron in its holster, unless you want us both killed here and now.'

Whit somehow complied, and sat on his horse, gripping his saddle-horn in sheer terror.

'I don't like this, Tom,' he wailed.

'Neither do I, Whit.'

They were soon surrounded by the *vaqueros* and looking down the barrels of numerous pistols.

Whit gave his brother a long, hard glare. 'I reckon this was not one of your best ideas, Tom.'

'Shut the hell up, boy,' Tom Hardy snapped. He had a feeling that for once his kid brother might just be right.

TWENTY-ONE

Darkness had arrived exactly on cue. Leaving the black stallion tied up to a dead white tree-stump, Iron Eyes had entered the mountain range on foot, carrying his Winchester over his back on a leather strap. Bats swooped around his head and their high-pitched squeaking filled his ears. The half moon overhead gave him ample light to see and not be seen, as he moved up and over the rounded rock formations which looked as if they had fallen off the moon itself.

Storm clouds in the distance seemed to be heading in the direction of the mountain range, and lightning flashes lit up the far-off prairie. Iron Eyes hoped that the storm would catch up with him before he caught up with the bandits. The confusion of a violent storm never hurt his chances.

This was no normal place, he thought. This was a place of danger. His nostrils filled with the aroma of distant humans. Humans always left a smell on the air, wherever they dwelled. It was the stench of dirt. Human dirt.

Iron Eyes pulled out both his loaded Navy Colts and gripped them firmly, as his long legs took him up across the tops of the rocks.

Higher and higher he climbed. He had the agility of a puma as he hopped from one huge boulder to the next.

It was as if he had some in-built ability to be drawn to whomever he was pursuing. Below him, the canyon floor wound into many forks. Some gaining altitude whilst others stayed almost level. These were the dried-up remains of ancient river-beds. Climbing above these sandy trails and using the rocks to cross the great distances of the vast mountain range, Iron Eyes knew that he would have more chance of spotting the bandits before they spotted him.

The shadows were interlocking amid the rounded rocky peaks that seemed to go on forever. Iron Eyes used every one of those shadows to move further into the heart of the mountains.

Suddenly, he saw the lone sentry ahead of him. A fat, small man with a battered sombrero sitting upon a large rock, wrapped in a thick blanket. Between his legs he held his trusty rifle.

Iron Eyes pushed both his guns into his belt, and drew out a long, thin stiletto from inside his left boot. The sharp blade fitted neatly between his broken teeth as he crept on all fours up the smooth rock-face, toward the seated sentry.

It was almost as if he were a phantom. Iron Eyes could move without making a single noise. This was an art that he had perfected over a dozen or more years of his grisly trade.

Iron Eyes was suddenly behind the sentry. Removing the blade from his mouth, he swiftly drove it deeply into the man's heart, with enough force to break several ribs. He screwed the blade around as if gutting a fish, before pulling the blood-soaked stiletto from the man's body.

The fat man's life had ended silently.

Iron Eyes wiped the blade on the dead man's blanket, before sliding it back into his boot. Then he continued his quest as if nothing had happened.

Deeper and deeper he penetrated the mountain fortress. Then he could hear them as well as smell them.

Crouching down, Iron Eyes edged forward over the rocks and boulders until he was at a point several hundred feet above the camp.

For a moment he just lay upon his flat stomach staring down at the scene below his vantage point.

A blazing fire set between the small group of wooden shacks illuminated the entire area. It was like a miniature town. The wine must have been flowing, he thought, as he watched the revelry below him. None of the people he watched seemed able to walk properly. They were staggering from one depraved activity to another.

Staring about the opposite rock-faces he looked for more sentries. There were none.

Iron Eyes focused hard on the scene below him as he started his gradual descent through the rocks and dark shadows. The thunder seemed to be getting closer, as he could smell the freshness in the air he breathed. He knew that the storm was heading toward the bandits' camp. Iron Eyes prayed that he would have time to reach the canyon floor before the storm arrived. There was nothing worse than trying to climb down a rock-face that was lashed with rain.

He did not relish the thought of losing his footing and sliding down two hundred feet of solid rock.

Although dark, the moonlight made everything appear blue. Only the bandits' campfire contained any true colours. Iron Eyes moved like a big cat toward the dozens of people who were totally unaware of his approaching.

Every few minutes the sky lit up with the flashing of nature's electricity. The sound of rumbling thunder grew louder as it started to echo around the canyon walls. Yet none of the bandits or their women seemed to give a damn. They just carried on with their festivities.

The descent took over thirty minutes, but the bounty-hunter knew he had to move slowly, using every shadow as a shield. He was hopelessly outnumbered yet this only increased his determination to complete his task.

Iron Eyes had tasted blood once this evening, and knew that he wanted more. Killing human vermin was the only thing that he was any good at. He knew that it was an evil trade, but to him it was totally justified.

Some folks could only be cured by death. After dying, they never repeated their mistakes.

The floor of the canyon was flat, as if pressed by an unseen, giant hand. As he reached it, Iron Eyes slid behind a large boulder and sat in the black shadow, getting his wind back.

Behind him he could hear the noise of drunken bandits and their women having a good time. That sort of happiness had always eluded the bounty-hunter. For him, nothing was that simple. As he sat in the dark shadows he checked his guns once more.

Across the way, a crude corral held over two dozen horses of various types. Some looked good and others scrawny, very much like the bandits themselves.

Another flash, and a deafening explosion of thunder shook the entire area around him.

Then the dark clouds drifted over the roof of the canyon and blocked out the moonlight. The raindrops that followed were warm and sparse. Using the additional darkness to his advantage, Iron

Eyes rose to his feet and ran silently toward the shack on the outermost edge of the camp. Then the rain became heavier and cooler.

As the rain hit the large campfire it began to hiss like an outraged diamond-back, sending plumes of smoke around the area. None of this seemed to have any effect on the bandits or their women as they continued to enjoy their drunken orgy.

The tall bounty-hunter moved silently behind the coarse shacks, staring into the open doorways and windows as he passed. He had never witnessed such open displays of uninhibited carnal activities before. It was as if he had fallen into a Tombstone whorehouse.

Yet nothing he saw had the slightest effect upon him. It was as if he had never had such feelings himself. There was nothing in his heart except death.

His was a black soul. Void of humanity.

Still holding his pistols tightly in his bony hands, he found the shack that he had sought for several minutes. Staring through the small hole that pretended to be a window, he spied a small, huddled form cowering like a whipped dog in a corner. At first he thought she was just another of the camp women. Then the terrible truth dawned upon him.

This was Maria Valdez.

This tortured creature was the daughter of Dwan José.

Iron Eyes leaned back into the shadows as his heart raced. It was not that he had never seen cruelty before. He was guilty of inflicting it upon others in his time himself. Yet not like this.

Crawling through the sand, he moved around the shack to get a better look at the crowd.

The rain was now sweeping across the dancing, drinking souls, who stayed close to their huge fire. Logs were being tossed on to its red heart, keeping its flames well nourished. The yellow light that flickered lit up the men and women. Iron Eyes studied each and every male face that he could see. He had the wanted poster image in his mind, and was searching the many faces for a match.

Then he saw the man that he had been hunting.

The Snake was drinking his fill, and grabbing every female that came close enough to his strong hands.

The gold tooth glinted in the light of the fire as the rain fell around the canyon. Steam rose off the gathering as they continued their revelry.

Iron Eyes gritted his teeth as he moved back to the small window. Getting to his feet, he removed his long coat and rifle before dropping them silently to the ground. Then he pushed one of his Navy Colts into his belt, whilst retaining the other in his left hand. He used his long legs to step up into the window, and fell silently into the dark, stinking shack.

Maria's sobbing sent cold chills through his spine as he crouched below the window. His eyes darted from the doorway to the girl and then back again. Slowly, he moved toward her.

TWENTY-TWO

The *hacienda* was its usual brightly lit self. That was the only thing that seemed normal on this night.

This was an evening filled with worry and concern.

Dwan José Valdez had not trusted either of the strange men his *vaqueros* had brought to him at gunpoint a few hours earlier. It was strange for this most generous of men to distrust anyone, but the Hardy brothers just brought out the worst in the elderly gentleman.

He had supplied them with food and with wine, but not with the things that he normally provided. These were men that did not seem worthy of his trust. Therefore he did not give them any.

The *vaqueros* had removed all the Hardy brothers' weapons before bringing them into the *hacienda* courtyard.

Valdez had ordered them not to be left

unguarded. He had more on his mind than two stray drifters. His thoughts were with the tall, shadowlike Iron Eyes.

Tom and Whit were treated well. The brothers had their horses groomed, watered and fed by Valdez's stable hands.

Supplies were given to them freely, before Dwan José Valdez came to the small tack room where they were being kept.

'You are free to go on your way,' Valdez started to tell the two rough riders, 'as long as you leave my property and head back across the border.'

Tom gazed up at the old man, who was flanked by his heavily armed *vaqueros*. 'You ordering us out of Mexico?'

'I am.' Valdez's eyes narrowed.

'What the hell for?' Tom felt insulted.

'Because we have enough filth in our country without stealing more from yours.' The elderly man was in no mood to argue with anyone.

'Can he kick us out of Mexico, Tom?' Whit Hardy was still enjoying the free wine that had been provided by their host.

'I can do anything I want,' Valdez interrupted.

'Guess we are leaving,' Tom shrugged.

'We have seen to your horses. They are fresh now, and able to carry you back home.' Valdez turned to leave the tack room, when he was stopped by a question that struck him unexpectedly.

135

'You heard of a critter named Iron Eyes?' Tom Hardy asked.

Valdez kept his back to the men. 'I think you will leave my *hacienda* very quickly.'

'How come, old-timer?' Tom stood and smiled at the back of his host.

Dwan José turned. 'Otherwise my men will shoot you and bury you out in the sand for the ants to eat.'

Whit jumped to his feet and grabbed his older brother's arm in terror.

'What's wrong, boy?' Tom asked.

'Shut the hell up, Tom. These folks ain't civilized like us.'

Tom shook his head at the floor.

'You still scared of ants, Whit?' he sighed.

TWENTY-THREE

The Snake had no idea of what lay in waiting for him as he headed drunkenly back to his shack and the awaiting Maria.

Pushing his way through the bandits and the females, the man with the golden tooth began to stagger as he walked. Pausing for only a brief moment to finish off yet another black glass bottle of wine, he burped before proceeding.

As he entered the dark room, he closed the door behind him. He felt around for the shelf where he kept his matches and found them. Striking a match, he touched the naked wick of his lantern and watched as the glowing filled every corner of the shack.

Speaking his drunken words of passion he headed for the corner where she huddled under the stinking blanket.

As his soiled hands pulled the blanket off her, his bloated face suddenly went very pale.

The sight that met his puffy eyes made him reel

back in a mixture of shock and fear. He had heard of a man who fitted this *gringo*'s description.

'Howdy, Snake,' Iron Eyes grinned, as he held a Navy Colt on the bandit leader. Maria Valdez hid herself behind the seated bounty-hunter.

The Snake dropped the blanket and tried to speak without success. His throat was dry from shock.

Iron Eyes got to his feet, and hauled the shaking Maria up after him. She stayed behind her tall saviour, unable or unwilling to face the man known as the Snake.

'You look pretty shook up, Snake.'

'You are Iron Eyes,' the bandit muttered.

'You know of me?' Iron Eyes poked the man in his ample belly with the barrel of his pistol. 'I'm flattered.'

'You will die this night, *Señor* Iron Eyes,' the Snake snarled at the bounty-hunter.

'Possibly.' Iron Eyes felt it was a pretty good bet that this was one game he would not win.

'Why you do this?' The Snake was defiant as he swelled up his chest, trying to scare the man who knew no fear.

'Do what?'

'Come here?'

'I got a couple of very good reasons,' Iron Eyes replied, with a sound in his voice that came from somewhere low in his soul.

'I heard that you were smart, but to come here

138

is very stupid.' The Snake was trying to stand his ground, and Iron Eyes admired that.

'I like being stupid, Snake,' Iron Eyes growled. 'It makes killing rats like you more fun.'

'I think you will not get out of my camp alive.' The Snake indicated to the door. 'I have many men and they are all very good with their guns. We had to kill twenty *vaqueros* to capture Valdez's daughter.'

'I heard it was eight *vaqueros*, Snake,' Iron Eyes corrected the bandit. 'And your men are pretty damn drunk.'

'Maybe it was eight.' The Snake raised his eyebrows. 'But you still have not explained why you come here to certain death.'

The bounty-hunter pushed the bandit leader down on to a chair, and rammed the gun into his mouth.

'This answer your question?' Iron Eyes asked, as he reached down and pulled out a long stiletto from the inside of his boot.

As the Snake was about to nod he felt something. Something that he had never experienced before. Something being pushed into his guts and forced up into his heart. Before he was able to work out that it was the blade of Iron Eyes' stiletto, his depraved life ceased with a loud, gushing sound. The face suddenly went blank as it sucked on to the barrel of the pistol.

Iron Eyes pulled his gun barrel out of the lifeless mouth and wiped the spit and dribble off on to his shirt.

Then, putting the long barrel of his Navy Colt into his belt, he tugged hard to remove the knife from the Snake's torso. Blood squirted over the floor and Iron Eyes' boots. Both he and the silent Maria watched as the body slid off the hard chair and on to the shack floor.

The bounty-hunter watched the dead man for several seconds before he felt a hand on his shoulder.

'Who are you?' Maria whispered.

'They call me Iron Eyes, Miss,' Iron Eyes replied, as he went down on one knee and poked the still-bloody blade into the open mouth of the Snake.

There was a cracking sound before the bounty-hunter's fingers retrieved something covered in blood. Wiping it on the bandit's clothing, he showed the small object to the young female.

It was the gold tooth.

'What do you want with that?' she gasped in horror.

'Trophy for your pop,' he replied, getting back to his feet.

Maria Valdez spat on the dead man, before kicking him with all the rage she had been withholding for ten long days. Her prayers had been answered, but she was still in the dirty shack and a long way from freedom and safety. Could this man who had killed the Snake so easily, really get her out of this evil place?

She watched as he moved to the door and peered through the ill-fitting frame. The rain had eased up, but the revelry remained almost as frantic as before.

'Now what?' Maria asked in his ear.

'I'm thinking.'

TWENTY FOUR

The *vaqueros* pointed the way back to the Rio
Grande and then rode away, leaving Whit and
Tom Hardy alone in their saddles under the
black, stormy sky. Lightning flashes lit up the
distant mountains and spooked their mounts.

'Well?' Tom Hardy sat leaning on his horse's
neck.

'We gonna go back to Texas?' Whit asked, trying
to see in the dark evening gloom.

'What the hell for?' Tom sniffed. 'We came to do
a job and we is gonna do it.'

Whit reached into his saddle-bags and withdrew a bottle of wine, pulling the cork out with his
teeth. 'You are still crazy.'

Tom felt angry. 'I wanna avenge Dan's murder,
boy.'

'Then I gotta say "*adios*", Tom.' Whit swigged at
his bottle, and gulped down the bitter-sweet fluid.
'Get killed on your own if you like. I am getting as
far away from here as this nag will take me.'

Tom rounded his horse to be face on with his younger brother.

There was a long silence between the two men as they stared at one another in the darkness. A partial moon and a few stars were all that lit up the scene. It was enough.

'What about heading north?' Tom suggested reluctantly.

'We could go straight.' Whit grinned as he offered what was left of his bottle to his sibling.

'Pigs might fly.' Tom grabbed the bottle and downed what was left of the wine, before tossing the bottle away.

The two men steered their horses north at a pace that was slow enough to guarantee an easy, painless ride.

Neither man believed the other that their business with Iron Eyes was truly finished. They just rode away from the *vaqueros* and Dwan José Valdez.

They had plenty of time.

TWENTY FIVE

Iron Eyes had managed to get the weak, beaten Maria Valdez out of the filthy shack, leaving the very dead Snake behind and picking up his Winchester. He checked that the repeating carbine was still operational before donning his long heavy coat once more. His icy glare froze the situation before them. There were just too many people around that damn campfire. Tapping her small shoulder, exposed by the tear across her dress where it had been torn from her body by the evil bandit, Iron Eyes moved his head in a gesture that told her to follow him. It was a long way around the back of the shacks to the corral, but it was a journey that they both had to endure.

As she followed the silent man she wondered who or what he was, to risk his life for a total stranger. His lank, wet hair covered his face most of the time, as he moved holding his rifle firmly across him, ready to use it at a split-second's notice.

Briefly, he had thought that they might retrace his route into the camp, but the rain still fell and the mountain slopes that surrounded the canyon were running with fresh rain-water and impossible to climb.

Iron Eyes knew that they had but one chance, and that was to get to the horses.

Whether they would be able to ride out of the hell-hole without being killed was doubtful. Yet it was his only plan, and he could not see any other option open to them.

She followed the tall, thin, ghostlike creature as he silently moved behind the small wooden dwellings. She had never been so tired as she was at this moment.

The days of being abused and kept a prisoner had taken their toll upon her frail, bruised body.

Sensing that she was weaker than he had at first thought, Iron Eyes stopped and returned to her. He put an arm under her shoulder and lifted her off her feet, then continued with her hanging off him.

She was lighter than he had at first thought. There seemed to be no excess flesh upon her entire body. He wondered if she were like himself, one of those people who seldom ate and seemed able to exist upon fresh air and liquor. Then he remembered who she was and what her pedigree was.

Iron Eyes had never been so close to a real lady

before, and felt angry that she was hurt.

She had been starved and beaten by the Snake for ten days, and in the heat of the shack, in the blistering Mexican climate, she had just sweated off all her body fat.

Maria felt as if she were floating as they moved to the edge of the last shack before stopping. Her eyes stared at the side of his face, and wondered why he was so cold. It was a scarred face, which had seen many battles.

Iron Eyes put a thin finger to her lips as if ordering her to remain silent. She watched as he strained to hear every sound that came from the surrounding area. He sniffed the cool breeze as if he could detect things by their sheer scent alone.

Iron Eyes was a hunter.

He knew things that most men never learn. He did not have to rely upon what his incredible vision could see. He used all his senses. It was said of Iron Eyes that he had the ability to smell danger. It might have just been a legend, but he was almost that good at what he did.

The rain continued to fall as they waited at the edge of the last shack. He held her up with one arm as his hand gripped the trigger of his Winchester in the other.

Maria was getting concerned as he released his grip on her and gently rested her against the wooden wall. He put his finger to his own lips and sank down in a crouching position.

She watched as the rain beat off his head, sending his long, limp hair hanging like damp string over his face. Yet his face remained frozen as he concentrated upon something.

Maria wondered how he could let the rain hit his eyes without ever blinking. Then she became aware of what he had been expecting.

A drunken bandit staggered around the corner into the black shadows, stood with his sombrero over his eyes and pulled down the front of his loose pants to get rid of some of the wine he had been consuming. The man was totally unaware of either Maria or Iron Eyes' proximity.

Iron Eyes moved like a wild puma at the man, bringing him down quickly and silently. The rifle butt was used and then the stiletto. The tall bounty-hunter dragged the body through the mud before dumping it behind the shack.

Maria watched as he returned to her side as if nothing had happened. This was a man who killed without any guilt. It was a natural reflex to Iron Eyes. However much it frightened her she owed her life to him. Loyalty and trust now consumed her, taking away some of the heartbreak that the Snake had inflicted upon her body and soul during the past ten days.

'Can we get out of this place?' she whispered softly. 'Can we ever escape?'

His grey eyes seemed to radiate as he looked down at her for a brief moment. 'We just might.'

147

Then he concentrated upon the small structure to the side of the crudely constructed corral, and pointed at it.

'Any idea what they got in there?'

She shook her head. 'I do not know.'

He slid his arm under her shoulder once more, lifted her off the ground and ran across to the fence rails that held the horses back. They both clambered through the poles and moved to the small, three-sided building. It was a dark place, filled with saddles and bridles. At the far end two boxes were stacked, one on top of another.

Iron Eyes moved quickly and used his knife to prise off the nailed-down lid of the top box. Maria Valdez watched in confusion as he removed the top box and then opened the bottom box.

'What is it?' she asked, as her attention was drawn to the fire and the dancing people a hundred yards away.

'Dynamite and fuses,' he replied, filling one of his coat pockets with the deadly sticks of explosives and the other with the fuses.

As he moved toward her she stepped nervously back, as if afraid that they would both be blown up.

'It's safe,' he said, bluntly pushing her down on to a small stool to rest, whilst he grabbed two saddles and bridles off the large stack.

'What are you going to do?' she asked, feeling even weaker than earlier.

148

Iron Eyes had no time to answer. He busied himself with two of the less timid horses, saddling them for their escape. The man who looked closer to death than any other human being she had ever encountered led the creatures to the front rail and tied their reins firmly. He had hatched a crude plan that had all the elements required for success, yet was unlikely to work given their situation.

For the first time, Iron Eyes stopped and leaned over her and talked straight and true.

He had to give her information about what he was going to attempt. She had her part to play, although he doubted that she could play any part at all given her state.

Slowly he spoke to her as the rain beat down upon his long hair. Maria Valdez was using every ounce of her inner strength to listen and remember his instructions.

All she could think about was the long fuses that were sticking out from his coat pocket and the steam that was rising from him.

TWENTY-SIX

Like a human cat, Iron Eyes had spent the next hour using the cover of every shadow he could find in the canyon to move around without being spotted by any of the bandits or their women. It had taken nearly sixty minutes to plant every stick of dynamite and insert various lengths of fuse wire into them.

Now he had placed the final primed stick under the end shack where the dead body of the Snake lay.

It was all guess-work now, as Iron Eyes reached inside to his shirt pocket and pulled out his dry box of matches and a long, thin cigar.

He lit his cigar and inhaled the strong blue smoke. Then he removed it from his mouth and blew the ash until it glowed red.

The guess-work was how long each and every fuse would take to reach the dynamite sticks. He had no idea whether they were slow or fast fuses.

All he knew was that they were each three feet long.

Touching the burning tip of the cigar to the first fuse wire, he waited until it started to hiss and burn before he rushed to the next planted stick and lit that too. Iron Eyes repeated this action ten times before he was standing at the end shack opposite the corral where the injured Maria Valdez and the two saddled horses awaited.

Just as he was about to run across the gap to them, a door opened behind him. Iron Eyes span around on his heels and moved instinctively at the figure in the darkened doorway.

To his utter surprise as he grabbed at the figure, he realized that this was a small, round woman. She was naked from the waist up and had breasts that seemed to reach her navel.

It was too late to stop himself, and he found himself tackling the creature to the ground. She was pretty drunk and her breath hit him as hard as a good left hook.

As they hit the ground he could see that she seemed to be quite enjoying this wrestling match and was clinging at his collar with her small strong fingers.

Casting his eyes across at the edge of the shack where he had planted the final dynamite stick he could see that the fuse was half gone which meant that the first must be almost ready to explode.

Iron Eyes clenched his fist and hit the woman

as hard as he could, squarely upon the tip of her chin. As his knuckles met her jaw he heard and felt the bone break inside her skull. Her arms fell on to the ground as he gathered himself up and started running toward the corral.

Maria was mounted upon the smallest horse as he had instructed her earlier. When he got there, he quickly pulled the poles away from the edge of the simple corral.

Rushing to the other saddled horse, Iron Eyes mounted by leaping on to it. Grabbing not only his own reins but Maria's as well, he rode behind the herd of nervous horses and started to force them out into the canyon. The horses raced through the rain toward the now small glowing campfire and the few remaining bandits, with Iron Eyes and Maria in close pursuit.

The horses could smell freedom and were heading for it. Then as the first few horses passed the end shack, the first stick of dynamite exploded in furious horror.

The bandits were totally confused, and they rushed around, seeking out their weapons. The second and third sticks exploded almost five seconds after the first. Bodies and parts of bodies flew up into the night sky as more horses stampeded in terror around the scene. Iron Eyes shot feverishly at any bandits who dared to raise their weapons in his direction. When his first Navy Colt was empty he pushed it into his deep pocket and drew his other gun. Then three more explosions went off behind Iron Eyes and his young companion. Some of the bandits were shooting at anything and everything, whilst further blasts rocked the area, sending their kinsmen to hell.

As Iron Eyes rode he used his Navy Colt to shoot any remaining bandits that were still standing. His aim was still as deadly as ever, even when upon a galloping horse frightened by the noise and blinding explosions.

Their mounts followed the few loose horses that were heading out of the box canyon. Then behind them the shock waves of the last dynamite blasts almost drove their horses' noses into the muddy ground as they pressed onward.

Iron Eyes rode as he had never ridden before after the stray horses. He knew they would lead them out of this maze and into the flat prairie where he had left the large black stallion.

As the sun was starting to rise before them and its bright light swept across the desert, they emerged from out of the mountain range.

Iron Eyes pulled his mount to a halt and held up his arm holding the reins of Maria's mount. The two horses cantered to a stop as the long shadows caused by the morning sun warmed their bones.

She was lying with her head almost next to her mount's mane as she felt his strong hands lifting her from the saddle.

Then her weary eyes saw the proud black stallion, which she recognized as being one of her father's prized horses.

'Pepe!' she called to the stallion, as Iron Eyes carried her toward it.

The elegant head of the thoroughbred turned and snorted mutual recognition.

Iron Eyes lifted her up into the beautiful saddle upon the graceful horse, and stepped back to watch her. He watched as she sat there patting and talking to the black horse. He did not dwell upon what had happened to her before he had managed to get into the bandits' stronghold, although he was certain that she was marked for the remainder of her life.

He went back and mounted the bandits' pony that had carried him to safety, and rode up to her.

She looked down upon him from the high-shouldered stallion as he sat upon the smaller horse. It seemed quite strange to the tired girl to be back upon the back of her favourite horse, and finally she knew that she was indeed free once again. The vermin were destroyed by this thin man who said little but did much.

'Come on, Miss Valdez,' he said as he spurred his horse forward. 'Your poppa is waiting for you back at the *hacienda*.'

Suddenly as she rode the familiar horse after the strange ghostlike man, she felt a tear rolling down her cheek. For the first time in ten days she was shedding tears of happiness and joy.

TWENTY SEVEN

Iron Eyes stood alone in the lovely courtyard of Dwan José Valdez's *hacienda*. He had done everything and more for the man who owned this place and much more. Yet he was feeling grim reality burning into his very soul.

He had washed the blood off his face and boots, but it remained as a stain on his memory.

The gold tooth that he had plucked out of the Snake's dead mouth had been accepted by his elderly host with glee. The evil had been vanquished in this beautiful land. If any of the bandits were still in the land of the living, it was doubtful if they would ever show their faces anywhere near this place.

The gold that was bulging in his saddle-bags seemed somehow worthless to the tall bounty-hunter, as he dwelled upon the lanterns that were being lit around the courtyard as night once more approached.

His Apache pony was saddled and ready, even though he had been invited to stay for as long as he wished. Iron Eyes was ready to leave this place.

Jane had left the *rancho* whilst he had been away, and taken her ox-drawn wagon to a place where she hoped to find something resembling happiness. The tall ghost of a man felt a mixture of anger and sadness at her leaving before his return. What she had feared was that the strange man with a chunk out of his ear would not return. By leaving this beautiful place she would never have to be told that Iron Eyes had been killed in his attempt to rescue Maria Valdez.

The cigar was a good, relaxing smoke, and its thick smoke filled his lungs whilst he stood beside the pony. His reflection in the fountain water-trough showed a face that Iron Eyes did not recognize. This was a man who could never say what he meant or do what he wanted to do. He had chosen a trail that was paved with gold and little else. The reflection showed Iron Eyes as he had never seen himself.

Then he heard the distinctive footsteps coming down the tiled steps behind him. He knew it was Dwan José without even turning around to look at the man.

'You leave, my tall friend?' Valdez asked, placing a fatherly hand upon the bounty-hunter's shoulder.

Iron Eyes seemed unable or unwilling to make eye contact as he answered, 'Might as well go.'

'Why?' The elderly man seemed concerned for Iron Eyes, who had done him the greatest favour any man could do for another.

'I got places to go and people to hunt,' came the reply from the dry, thin lips. 'Besides, you say that the Hardy brothers were here. I might just try to catch up with them.'

'To kill them?' Valdez frowned.

'They got money on their heads too,' Iron Eyes said, with little fire in his voice. 'I might just collect that before someone else does.'

'Iron Eyes.' There was sadness in the older man's voice.

'Not that I'll try to catch up with them.'

Valdez was not convinced by the man's answer, and knew the true reason. 'You are sad, my tall one. It is because your Jane left here whilst you were saving my child, is it not?'

Iron Eyes grunted.

'Stay, *amigo*.' Valdez stepped in front of the taller man, forcing him to look into his face. 'Stay here. You are a hero to my people and myself. Stay.'

'Can't,' Iron Eyes said in a low voice. 'I gotta ride.'

'You go after Jane?'

'Nope,' Iron Eyes replied. 'She don't need me and I don't need her.'

'But she was so concerned about you, my friend.'

'Then why did she light out?' Iron Eyes felt betrayed by the woman with the wagon.

'She was angry at me for asking you to save my daughter,' Dwan José answered. 'I think she was terrified that you would be killed and she could not face that.'

Iron Eyes untied his reins from the hitching-pole, and stared at the beautiful *hacienda*. 'You got a fine place here, Dwan José.'

Valdez watched as the bounty-hunter mounted slowly. 'You are a strange man.'

'Because I have no woman?'

'Because you turn away from those who care, Iron Eyes.' The words of the elderly ranch-owner were closer to the truth than either of them could admit.

'I ain't got nothing but my guns, Dwan José.' Iron Eyes rested his hands upon the handles of his weapons and tried to look impressive.

'Stay here and you will never have to lift a finger again.'

Iron Eyes puffed on the cigar. 'I like lifting my fingers.'

'You will continue hunting men and killing them?'

'It's what I do.'

'You go to catch up with Jane?'

'Which way did she head?' Iron Eyes sucked on

the cigar and blew out the smoke.

'She headed north toward the border.' Valdez walked beside the man as he rode slowly toward the arched gateway. 'You can catch up with her very quickly, I think.'

Iron Eyes patted the saddle-bags. 'Thank you for the gold, Dwan José.'

'Thank you for giving me back my Maria, *amigo*.' Valdez stopped as the tall rider paused for a moment before looking down at him.

'I think that little lady got hurt real bad by the Snake.'

'This I understand.' Valdez bowed his head in regret.

'They paid the price.' Iron Eyes nodded as he puffed upon his cigar. 'I made them pay the price in full.'

'Thanks to you,' Dwan José reached up and shook the bounty-hunter's hand, 'she is now safely home.'

'You better keep an eye on her,' Iron Eyes advised. 'I seen women go loco after that sort of thing.'

'My Maria is strong.'

'No woman is that strong.' Iron Eyes flicked the ash off his cigar. 'They just pretend to be.'

There was silence from both men for a moment. Then the older man watched as the lone rider spurred his mount and rode into the dusky desert.

The sun was setting and the sky was burning

as red as hell itself above their heads. As the phantom-like man rode, he raised a fist to the sky and yelled out to the watching Mexican.

'The sky's on fire.'

'*Si*, my tall friend,' Dwan José Valdez agreed. 'The sky is on fire.'

Iron Eyes drove his spurs into his mount's flesh, and the horse started to move faster into the wilderness.

Dwan José Valdez shook his head as he realized that Iron Eyes was not heading north after the woman named Jane. Iron Eyes was heading east, after the Hardy brothers. If he caught up with them he might just send them to where he had sent their late brother.

There was always room for one more outlaw in hell.

Soon the dust rose behind the hooves of the Indian pony, and the lonely bounty-hunter was no longer visible to the tired old man.

Riding with death as his only companion, and the smell of blood in his nostrils, Iron Eyes was gone.